Robert Grant

Search-Light Letters

Robert Grant

Search-Light Letters

ISBN/EAN: 9783743441743

Manufactured in Europe, USA, Canada, Australia, Japa

Cover: Foto ©Andreas Hilbeck / pixelio.de

Manufactured and distributed by brebook publishing software (www.brebook.com)

Robert Grant

Search-Light Letters

Search-Light
Letters

BY

Robert Grant

Contents

¶

To *A Young Man or Woman* in Search of
the Ideal

Letter I	1
Letter II	15
Letter III	32
Letter IV	45

¶

To *A Modern Woman* with Social Ambitions

Letter I	59
Letter II	72
Letter III	89
Letter IV	105

¶

To *A Young Man* wishing to be an American

Letter I	125
Letter II	135
Letter III	152
Letter IV	169

¶

To *A Political Optimist*

Letter I	173
Letter II	191
Letter III	214

To *A Young Man or Woman* in Search of the Ideal. I.

I SHALL assume certain things to begin with. If a young man, that the dividing-line between mine and thine is so clearly defined to your own consciousness that you are never tempted to cross it. For instance, that it is your invariable practice to keep the funds of others in a separate bank-account from the money which belongs to you, and not to mix them. That you will not lie to escape the consequences of your own or others' actions. That you are not afraid to stand up and be shot at if necessary. That you do not use your knife to carry food to your mouth; say "How?" for "What?" or hold the young lady whom you are courting or to whom you are engaged by the crook of her elbow and shove her along the street as though she were a perambulator. If a young woman, that you are so pure in thought that you do not feel obliged to read diseased fiction in order to enlighten yourself as to what is immorality. That you do not bear false witness against your neighbor by telling every unplea-

[1]

sant story you hear to the next person you meet. That you do not repeat to an acquaintance, on the plea of duty, the disagreeable remarks or criticisms which others have made to you regarding her. That you try to be unselfish, sympathetic, and amiable in spite of everything. That you neither chew gum nor use pigments. And that you do not treat young men as demigods, before whom you must abase yourself in order to be exalted.

I take it for granted that you have reached the moral and social plane which this assumption implies. Manners are, indeed, a secondary consideration as compared with ethics. A man who eats with his knife may, nevertheless, be a hero. And yet, it is not always easy to fix where manners and ethics begin. Many a finished young woman who stealthily heightens the hue of her complexion and blackens her eyebrows with paint probably regards the girl who chews gum with superior scorn. Yet tradition associates paint rather than gum with the scarlet woman. To avoid introducing the subtleties of discussion where all is so clear, it is simpler to exclude the use of either as a possible characteristic of fine womanhood. The homely adage that you cannot make a silk purse out of a sow's ear is full of meaning for democracy. Manners must go hand in hand with morals, or character will show no more lustre than the uncut and unpolished diamond, whose latent brilliancy is marred by uncouthness, so that it may readily be mistaken for a vulgar stone.

I assume, then, that you possess honesty, purity, and courage, the intention to be unselfish and sympathetic, and an appreciation of the stigma of vulgarity. If you are seeking the ideal, you will try to be, in the first place, an uncommon person. A common person is one who is content to be just like every one else in his or her own walk of life. The laws on our statute-books are made for the benefit of common people; that is to say, they are tempered to the necessities of the weak and erring. If you stop short there you will keep out of jail, but you will be a very ordinary member of society. This sounds trite, but the application of the principle involved is progressive. It is easy to be ordinary in the higher walks of civilization and yet pass for a rather superior person. It is only necessary to be content to "do as every one else does," and accept the bare limit of the social code under which you live as the guide of conduct.

[*Note*.—I am reminded here by my wife, Josephine, that, though the statute-laws are broken by few of our friends, there is one law which women who claim to be highly civilized and exceedingly superior are constantly breaking— the statute which forbids them to smuggle.]

¶ *Scene: An Ocean Steam-ship. Two sea-chairs side by side.*
¶ *Dramatis Personæ: A Refined and Gifted Instructress of Youth on the home passage from a summer's vacation abroad, and your Philosopher. A perfect sea and sky, which beget confidences.*

Refined and Gifted Instructress of Youth. It's rather a bother to have friends ask you to bring in things.

The Philosopher. I always say "Certainly; but I shall be obliged to declare them." That ends it.

Refined and Gifted. My friends wouldn't like that at all. It would offend them. You mustn't tell, but I have as commissions a dress, two packages of gloves, and a large French doll, in my trunk.

The Philosopher. Yet you will be obliged to sign a paper that you have nothing dutiable and that everything you have is yours.

Refined and Gifted. If I were to declare the things, the duties would all have to come out of my own pocket. I should n't have the face to collect it from my friends.

The Philosopher. They expect you to fib, of course. You prefer, then, to cheat the Government rather than disappoint persons who made use of you in order to accomplish that very thing?

Refined and Gifted. You don't put it nicely at all, Mr. Philosopher. Besides, the things are mine. I paid for them with my own money; and, until I am paid back, the things belong to me. There, now, why shouldn't I sign the paper?

The Philosopher. A shallow sophistry. A merchant who acted on that theory would be sent to jail. Will a refined and gifted instructress of youth, whose mission in life it is to lead the young in the paths of virtue, evade the law by a subterfuge?

Refined and Gifted. It's an odious law. My family all believe in free trade.

[5]

The Philosopher. Very possibly. But it is the law.

Refined and Gifted (after a pause). I don't care. If I declare the things they would never forgive me, and I can't afford to pay charges on their things myself. I've only just enough money to get home, anyway. Perhaps no one will ask me to sign it. By the way, how much ought I to give the man if he passes everything nicely?

The Philosopher. Nothing. That would be bribery.

Refined and Gifted. Why, I thought all men did that.

The Philosopher. Chiefly women who try to smuggle. *(Silence of five minutes.)*

Refined and Gifted. I don't care. I shall sign it.

And she did.

Those whose office it is to utter the last word over the dead rarely yield to the temptation to raise the mantle of charity and show the man or woman in all his or her imperfections. Society prefers to err on the side of mercy and forbearance, and to consign dust to dust with beautiful generalizations of hope and congratulation, even though the subject of the obsequies be a widely known sinner. However fitting it may be to ignore the truth in the presence of death, there can be no greater peril for one in your predicament than to cherish the easy-going doctrine that you are willing to take your chance with the rest of the world. The democratic proposition that every one is as good as his neighbor is readily amended so as to read that, if you are as good as your neighbor, everybody ought to be satisfied. A philosopher has a right to take liberties with the dead which a clergyman must deny himself. "Died at his late residence on the 5th inst., Solomon Grundy, in the sixty-seventh year of his age. Friends are kindly requested not to send flowers." Perhaps you saw it? Very likely you knew him. If so, you may have attended the funeral and heard read over his bier the beautiful words, "I heard a voice from Heaven which said, write Blessed are the dead who die in the Lord," and the hymn, which the family had requested, "Nearer, my God, to Thee." The officiating clergyman was not to blame. Solomon Grundy had worshipped at his church with regularity for twenty years, and had been

[7]

a fairly generous contributor to foreign and domestic missions, in spite of the fact that he had
the reputation down-town of being close as the
bark of a tree. The obituary notices in the newspapers referred to him as "a leading merchant"
and "a gentleman of the old school." No wonder that the Rev. Peter Tyson, who is a brave
man and has been known to rear on occasions,
felt that he could let himself go without injury
to his conscience. Besides, even so discriminating a person as your Philosopher saw fit to attend the funeral, and remembering that the old
gentleman had given him a wedding present,
would probably have ordered a wreath but for
the wishes of the family. And yet the facts of
Solomon Grundy's life, when examined in a
philosophic spirit, serve chiefly to point a moral
for one who is in search of the ideal. Read the
itinerary of his earthly pilgrimage and judge for
yourself:

Infancy (first six years).—No reliable data
except a cherubic miniature, and the family tradition that he once threw into the fire a neck-
lace belonging to his grandmother. People who
know all about such matters will tell you that
during these first six years the foundations of

character are laid. The miniature was always said to bear a striking resemblance to his maternal grandfather, who was a man of—nay, nay, this will never do. Those same people to whom I have just referred will tell you that we inherit everything we are, and, if I proceed on that theory, we are done with Solomon Grundy as soon as he was born. Decidedly a young man or woman in search of the ideal cannot afford to palm off on ancestors the responsibility for his or her own conduct.

Boyhood (six to sixteen).—So-called highly respectable surroundings and good educational advantages. Here we are brought face to face again with those same persons whom I have already instanced. *They* will assure you that Solomon's father and mother and his "environment" were the responsible agents during this period, and that whatever Solomon did not inherit or have settled for him before his sixth year was settled for him by them without the knowledge of said Solomon. This is rather discouraging as a study of Solomon as a conscious, active *ego*, but it affords you an opportunity, if you are not in search of the ideal, to make your parents and that comfortable phrase your "environment" bear the burden of all your short-comings until you are sixteen, and serve as an excuse for your shortcomings in the future.

Youth (sixteen to twenty-one).—Now we at least make progress. Solomon enters college. Gets one or two conditions, but works them off and stands erect. High spirits and corresponding consequences. Becomes popular and idle. Subscribes to the faith that the object of going to college is to study human nature, and is fascinated by his own acumen. Sudden revulsion at beginning of senior year. The aims and responsibilities of life unfold themselves in absorbing panorama, and his soul is full of high resolve. The world is his oyster. Studies hard for six months and graduates somewhat higher than had been anticipated. (Curtain descends to inspiring music.) Solomon stands on the threshold of life the image of virile youth, shading his brow and looking at the promised land.

Early Manhood (twenty-one to thirty).—Solomon decides to go into business. Reasons chiefly pecuniary. No special aptitude for anything else. Is sent abroad to study more human nature, acquire breadth of view and learn French. Does so in Paris. Returns with some of his high resolve tarnished, and with only a smattering of the language in question. Goes into the employ of a wholesale dry-goods merchant, and begins at the lowest round of the ladder. Works hard and absorbedly. Very little leisure. Devotes what he has to social diversion. Develops a pleasing talent for private theatricals, in the exercise of which falls in love with a pretty but impecunious young woman. (Slow and sentimental music.) Yearns to marry, but is advised by elderly business friends that he cannot afford it. Dejected winter in bachelor apartments. Takes up with Schopenhauer. Spirits slightly restored by first rise on ladder. Eschews society and private theatricals. Forms relations, which recall Paris, with sympathetic, nomadic young person. Gets another rise on the ladder, and is spoken of among his contemporaries as doing well.

Manhood (thirty-one to forty).—Works steadily and makes several fortunate investments. Joins one or two clubs, and gains eight pounds in weight. Grows side-whiskers or a goatee. Gets another rise, and the following year is taken into the firm. Complains of dyspepsia, and at advice of physician buys saddle-horse. Contributes fifty dollars to charity, joins a book-club and attends two political caucuses. Thinks of taking an active interest in politics, but is advised by elderly business friends that it would interfere with his business prospects. Owing to the death of a member of the firm, becomes second in command. Thinks of changing bachelor rooms and wonders why he shouldn't marry instead. Goes into society a little and looks about. Gains five extra pounds and makes more fortunate investments. Picks out good-looking, sensible girl eight years younger than himself, with a tidy property in her own right. Is conscious of being enraptured in her presence, and deems himself very much in love. (Orchestra plays waltz by Strauss.) Offers himself and is accepted. Burns everything in his bachelor rooms and sells out all his speculative investments. Regrets to observe that he is growing bald. Impressive ceremony and large wedding-cake.

Manhood — Middle Age (forty to fifty-five). — Conservative attitude toward domestic expenses. Works hard from what he calls "new incentive." Delights in the peacefulness of the domestic hearth. Blissful mental condition. (Religious music.) Buys pew in Rev. Peter Tyson's church. Buys baby-wagon. Increasing profits in dry-goods business. Almost bald. Gives two hundred dollars to foreign missions. Is proud of his wife's appearance and entertains in moderation. Becomes head of firm. Buys gold-headed cane and gains five more pounds. Goes to Europe for six months, with his wife, and conducts himself with propriety, visiting cathedrals and historical monuments. Shows her Paris. Foresees financial complications and turns ship accordingly. Increasing family expenses and depressing conditions in dry-goods trade. Completely bald. First attack of gout. Absorbed in business and in real-estate investments. On return of commercial prosperity, reaps the reward of foresight and sagacity. Is chosen director of two railroads and a trust company. Is elected president of his club. Gives five hundred dollars to domestic missions. Buys new house and a barouche for his wife. Gives large evening entertainment. Second attack of gout. Goes to Carlsbad for treatment. (Toccata by Galuppi.)

Old Age—(fifty-five to sixty-seven).—Addresses Christian association on " How to Succeed in Life." Is appointed trustee of a hospital and an art museum. Votes conservatively on every question. Is referred to in newspapers as "Hon. Solomon Grundy." Slight attack of paralysis. Becomes somewhat venerable in appearance. Deplores degeneracy of modern ideas. Retires from active business. More venerable in appearance. Second attack of paralysis and death.

And that was the end of Solomon Grundy. A highly respectable representative of a second-class man. The term suggests an idea. We have here no first, second, and third class railway carriages, as are found in England and other countries. But it would be interesting, from a philosophical point of view, to invent such a train for the occasion, and bestow our friends and acquaintances, and, indeed, society at large, according to their qualifications. You, of course, are desirous to know who are the persons entitled to travel first-class, in order that you may be introduced to them and avoid intimacy with the others, so far as is consistent with Christian charity and the mutual obligations of social beings. But let me first dip my pen in the ink again.

To *A Young Man or Woman* in Search of the Ideal. II.

BRACADABRA. Presto! Behold the train. The gates are opened and the people press in. There will not be much trouble with the third-class passengers. See how they take their proper places of their own accord. Some of them deserve to ride second-class quite as much as many who will be affronted at not being allowed to go first-class. Do you see that man? He is a commercial traveller, or drummer, and, naturally, early on the ground. He does n't hesitate or examine his ticket, but gets directly into a second-class smoking-car, settles himself, and puts on a silk cap. He knows that it is useless to ask for a first-class seat, and he is going to make the best of it (which is good philosophy). Very likely if you were sitting next to him he would utter some such cheery remark as, "It will be all the same a hundred years hence," and tell you a pat story to illustrate the situation. Did you happen to notice, though, the longing look he cast at the first-class coaches as he went by? I feel sure that down in his heart he is ready to admit that there are such things as ideals, after all, and he is making resolutions as to what he would do if he could live his life over again.

Did you notice that stout, fashionably dressed man who stopped and looked at me with a grin? He was trying it on, so to speak. He knew just as well as Tom Johnson, the drummer, that he had no right to travel first-class, but he thought I might admit him on the score of social prestige. He is one of the kindest-hearted of fellows — just the man to whom a friend would apply in a tight place, and I rather think he would be apt to help an enemy, unless it happened that something he had eaten for supper the night before had disagreed with him. He has the digestion of an ostrich, and he needs it, for his skin is full of oil, and whiskey, and tortured goose-liver, and canvas-back ducks, and pepper-sauce, and ripe Camembert cheese, and truffles, and Burgundy, and many other rich and kindred delicacies. He could tell four different vintages of champagne apart with his eyes shut, and he has honor at his club on account of it. His name is Howard Vincent. An illustrious-sounding name, is n't it? He inherits gout from both sides of the family. He does not know Tom Johnson, the drummer. They have moved in different social strata. But they belong to the same order of human beings. There! you notice, he asks Tom for a light, and they have begun to talk together. They are laughing now, and Tom is winking. I should n't wonder if they were making fun of the first-class passengers. Vincent has read more or less in his day, and he rather prides himself on what he calls keeping abreast of the times in the line of thought. See, they have opened the window, and are beckoning to me. Let us hear what they have to say.

Drummer. Ah, there, philosopher! You would n't let us in, and I guess you know your business. We 've had a good time in life, anyhow. If the religious folk are right, we shall be in it up to our necks. If they 're wrong, they 've been wasting a lot of valuable time.

Howard Vincent. We've ridden straight, at all events. (Vincent is an authority on sporting matters.) We have n't pretended to be something we were not. We've never cheated anybody, and we've never lied to anybody, and each, according to his light (this last qualification was for Tom's benefit), has been a gentleman. We've been men of the world, and we have found the world a reasonably satisfactory place. We're in no haste to leave it.

The Philosopher. And may I add, gentlemen, that each of you has a kind and generous heart?

Did you observe how pleased they looked when I said that? It was a little weak of me to say it, but I could not help it. Somehow, it is very difficult to be sufficiently severe to such easy-going, pleasant-natured fellows, who are content to take the world as they find it, laugh and grow fat. Moreover, Tom Johnson has for twenty years supported his old mother and invalid sister, and remained single as a consequence; and Howard Vincent has a habit of giving away delightful sums on Christmas Day without advertising the fact. How often, on the occasion of death, do we hear the aphorism that everything counts for nothing save the kindly deeds of the deceased, until one is tempted to believe that a genial commercial traveller, like our friend, with a benignant soul is more admirable and inspiring than a highly sensitive gentleman and scholar. Indisputably this is so if the gentleman and scholar lacks the humanity for which the other is conspicuous;

but, nevertheless, it behooves the soul in search
of the ideal to beware of the slough of mere
warm-heartedness. It is an attribute which, if
relied on too exclusively as a leavening force,
is readily made to subserve very ordinary purposes. The two Falstaffian men in the second-
class car belong there, even though you might
find their kindly ways and their stories attractive up to a certain point. They are of the class
of men who, more signally perhaps than any
other, bar the path of the world's progress toward the stars by means of the argument that
what has been must be, and that what is is
good enough. They are of the men who shrug
their shoulders when the hope is expressed that
the abuse of liquor may be lessened and finally
controlled; who sneer at the efforts of the police authorities to shut up all the houses of ill-
repute, on the ground that prostitution has
always existed and must always exist. (That it
will never become "unpopular," as the drummer would tell you in his breezy way.) As-
suredly, you need to be on your guard against
infatuation with those big, genial and (usually)
pot-bellied personages whose large hearts and
abundant charity and splendid appetites allow

them to discard as unworthy of a sensible man's regard everything but honesty, reading, spelling and arithmetic (add, in the case of Howard Vincent, a dash of accomplishments and agnostic philosophy), Worcestershire sauce and jests of custom-made humor. Blessed be humor. The man or woman without it is like a loaf of stale bread or a cup of brackish water. But to be content with the mere workaday world and its ways is like travelling perpetually with a grip-sack. When we open the grip-sack, what do we find? The barest necessaries of life, without a trace of anything which inspires or refines. I have no desire to betray the private affairs of any commercial traveller, or to imply that the Bible and Shakespeare are not occasionally to be found both in the kit of the travelling man and the English leather trunk of the more elegant man of fashion. I am simply cautioning you, my male correspondents, to beware of accepting as final your world as you find it. Nothing is more sure to make you a second-class person. Mere good-natured common-sense ("horse-sense," as our drummer would call it) is a useful virtue, but it would keep civilization ordinary to the crack of doom.

Ah! now we are likely to have trouble. Notice, please, the lady coming this way. How graceful and elegant she is. A delicate, refined face and bearing. See how she sidles off from the third and second-class passengers with an expression of distaste for them which suggests pain. She cannot bear coarse people. She believes herself to be an intellectual woman with serious tastes. She aims to be a spiritual person and she reads many essays—by Emerson, Matthew Arnold, Pater, and others. She is fond of history and politics; not of this country, because she claims that it is vulgar and lacks picturesqueness. But she can tell you all about the governments of Europe, and who is prime minister of or in authority in each of them. Democracy does not interest her. It seems to her to concern the affairs of dirty or common people; and she cares nothing for the great social questions of the age. They appear to her to clash with personal spirituality and culture. She is very sensitive. She has made a study of music, especially Wagner. She is very particular as to what she has to eat, but the grossness of men, as she calls it, offends her seriously. She believes herself to be not very strong physically, and she is nervous on the subject of arsenic in wall-papers and germs in drinking-water. She has retained her maidenly instincts to the last.

What is that you ask, madam? A seat in a first-class carriage. Excuse me, you cannot go in there. You belong in the second-class section of the train. Mistake? There is no mistake. I understand perfectly. I'm ready to take your word for it that you have read Dante in the original, and I know that you are

> *Chaste as the icicle*
> *That's curded by the frost from purest snow,*
> *And hangs on Dian's temple.*

(Doubtless you recall the quotation.) But you must stay out. Your ticket reads "Personal culture and individual salvation," and it entitles you to ride in any of those second-class cars. You don't like the passengers? I am very sorry, I'm sure, but my instructions are explicit. I was told to keep out all ladies of your kind, who think that the ideal is to be attained by hugging themselves to themselves (excuse the coarseness of the metaphor, madam) all their days in a hot-house atmosphere, and playing bo-peep with their own souls. You intend to write a letter about it to the Boston *Evening* ——? Oh, very well. You will have to ride second-class, all the same.

Enter a clergyman. This seems more promising.

Clergyman. Is this the first-class section? I think my seat must be in here.

Philosopher. First-class here, sir. Tickets, please. *(Aside to correspondent.)* A modest gentleman, forsooth.

Clergyman (stops fumbling in his pocket for his tickets and sniffs suspiciously). I smell tobacco. Is there a smoking-car on the first-class train?

Philosopher. There is for those who smoke.

Clergyman. An outrage, sir. An unchristian outrage. I suppose next that you will tell me that intoxicating fluids are sold there.

Philosopher. Yes, sir, to those who use them. All the first-class passengers understand the use of such things in moderation. They are not injured by them.

Clergyman. A flimsy argument, sir. Think of the example. I repeat it, sir ; think of the example. I protest against it, sir, as a crime against our highest civilization. I — I will have you removed

[23]

from office. You are not fit to hold your position.
I will see the governor about it immediately. I
—I——

Philosopher (to correspondent). He fancies that
he is arguing on the liquor question before a
board of police commissioners. *(To clergyman.)*
The gentleman will come to order.

Clergyman. I insist on having the smoking and
drinking car detached, or I will not ride on the
train.

Philosopher. You will not ride in the first-class
portion of it, in any event. Your ticket reads
" Well-intentioned but overbearing visionary
enthusiast." Come, sir, pass on, or, in spite of
your cloth, I shall be obliged to put you in
charge of an officer for disturbing the peace.

I was interrupted here by my wife, Josephine.
" Of course I understand," said she, " that he
was very overbearing, and I have heard you say
before that clergymen are more apt to lose their
temper before committees than most other people. But the poor man was desperately in earnest.
The whole thing means so much to him. He believes that the world will never be redeemed until liquor and tobacco are no longer used in it.

Do you mean that you really think this will never come to pass?"

" Never is a long time, my dear," said I.

" But you were discussing the ideal."

" To be sure. Have you ever considered the matter from the moderate-drinker and smoker's point of view? Brain-weary, muscle-tired men have, from generation to generation, found a glass of wine or spirit and a cigar a refreshment and a comfort. Neither agrees with some, and many abuse the use of both. Drunkenness among the poor and tippling among the rich are, perhaps, the greatest enemies of civilization ; and, consequently, there is a corps of many women and some men who cry out upon the use of alcohol as incompatible with the world's progress. This sentiment at the polls expresses itself chiefly in very small minorities, unless the voters are reasonably near to some large city or town. The failure of the movement to make important headway might be ascribed to the fact that the mass of people are still unenlightened, were there any signs that the intelligent workers of the world are disposed to side with the wearers of the white ribbon. The use of champagne, claret, brandy, and whiskey continues unabated over the civilized world, if one is to judge by economic statistics and trade circulars. They are quaffed on state and festal occasions, generally with moderation, by lords and ladies, statesmen, lawyers, doctors, bankers, soldiers, poets, artists, and often by bishops and clergymen. At ninety-nine out of every hundred formal dinner-parties in London, Paris, Berlin, or New York, alcohol is offered in some form to the guests as a stimulus to conversation, and, were it not so, there would be ninety-nine grumblers to every one man or woman who, at present, turns his or her glasses down with an ill-bred, virtuous air."

"And yet," said Josephine, "I have heard you say constantly that it would be no particular deprivation to you to give up wine."

"No more it would. In this country, with its stimulating climate, most nervous people are better for a very little if any alcohol, and many men are apt to find that it is simpler not to drink at all. But, remember, we are considering the question whether there is any reason why the man or woman in perfect health, and in search of the ideal, should be a teetotaler, and if there is any probability that the world will banish alcohol and cigars from the dignified occasions of the future. In other words, when the world has learned not to drink and smoke too much, will it cease to drink and smoke altogether? I know that the advocates of total-abstinence argue about the serenity and sane joy of a cold-water banquet, and it may be that we are a trifle hysterical in our declarations that conversation must lag until one has had a glass of champagne ; but is not much of the light, masculine laughter of life associated with the fruit of the grape and the aroma of tobacco? Have you ever tried to picture to yourself a world as it would be if there were well-enforced, rigid prohibition everywhere, and the tobacco-plant were no more?"

Josephine gave a little laugh. "You say the masculine laughter of the world. I assure you that much of the masculine laughter which you associate with the fruit of the grape is associated in the feminine mind with conjugal or maternal tears. I quite understand your appeal to the imagination from the masculine point of view. That is, I suppose the words wine and tobacco bring in their train for man many pleasing and even inspiriting images ; that under their influence the soldier believes himself more brave and wins battles in anticipation ; that the artist gets a glimpse of his great picture, and that the tired husband and father sees evolve from the bottom of his beer-mug a transfigured reflection of his wife and children. But we women, who, as a sex, have always done without wine and tobacco, know from experience that, however lofty and delightful your visions at such times, there is always a reaction after alcohol, and that we generally get the full benefit of the reaction. If, now, inspiring visions never came to us and other total-abstainers, there would seem to be some reason why we should be willing to bear the brunt of man's inebrieties a little longer; but really, my dear philosopher, is there any reason to believe that we do not entertain visions quite as inspiring and delightful as yours? We drink only tea—too much of it for our nerves, I dare say—but we will gladly give that up if you will abjure alcohol and cigars. There certainly is no poetry in the aroma of tobacco in the curtains, next day, and we pass the morning with it when you have gone down-town. Don't you think there is a great deal of humbug in the notion that in order to laugh lightly and remember gladly men need to be titillated either by wine or tobacco? I 'm glad you would n't allow that bumptious clergyman to ride in a first-class car, but I don't see why the world should not be just as gay, and many women twice as happy, if there were no wine or tobacco. Only think how light-hearted woman would be if the incubus of man's drunkenness, under which she has staggered for hundreds of years, should be lifted off forever! She would be so bubbling over with happiness that, even though as a consequence man were in the dumps and without visions, she would make him merry in spite of himself."

"Very likely, Josephine. I am disposed to agree with you that the jest and merriment of masculine youth would not be entirely and hopelessly repressed. But you do not take sufficiently into consideration—and in this you imitate the bumptious clergyman who was going to have me removed—the world's cravings and necessities as a world. If, pardon me, men were all women in their appetites, and life were one grand pastoral *à la* Puvis de Chavannes— if, in short, the world were not the bustling, feverish, perplexing, exhausting, crushing, cruel world, men would not crave stimulants to help them to do their work or to forget it. If there were no alcohol or cigars, would not those who now use either to excess have recourse to some other form of stimulant or fatigue and pain disguiser instead? Why should those who have learned the great lesson of life, self-control, renounce the enjoyment of being artificially strengthened or cheered because others let their appetites run away with them and make beasts of them? I have, indeed, already suggested that it is a dangerous argument to instance an existing state of affairs as a reason against change; but I beg to call your attention to the fact that the world seems to pay very little heed to the lamentations of the teetotalers, so far as total-abstinence is concerned. There has been a change of temper among all classes in the direction of moderation in the use of liquor and wine, and legislation regulating and restricting licenses is becoming popular. But if the wearers of the white ribbon were to make inquiries of the dealers in glass-ware, they would find that no fewer newly married couples, among the educated and well-to-do in every country, buy wine-glasses as a necessary table article, in order to provide wine or beer for those whom they expect to entertain. There are certainly no signs that society, in the best sense, has any intention of adopting prohibition as a cardinal virtue, but many signs that it is seriously determined to make warfare on inebriety, and no longer to proffer it the cloak of social protection when the offenders happen to be what the world used to call gentlemen. One's ideal should not be too remote from probable human conclusions, and it does not seem likely, from present indications, that man, unless he be persuaded that the moderate use of stimulants is seriously injurious to his health, will ever be willing to banish them from the markets of the world because a certain portion of the community has not the necessary intelligence or self-control to use them with discretion. As for tobacco, it is a long cry from now to the millennium, but a philosopher cannot afford, at this stage of the itinerary, to cut off the smoking-car from the first-class portion of the train, for by so doing he might confound even archbishops and other exemplary personages."

To *A Young Man or Woman* in Search of the Ideal. III.

I WAS interrupted at this point in my letter by the loud ringing of the front-door bell. Glancing at the clock, I observed that it was eleven. Consequently, the servants must have gone to bed. Under these circumstances, a philosopher has to open the front door himself, or submit to a prolonged tintinnabulation. "Ting-a-ling-a, ling-a-ling-a-ling" went the bell again.

"It must be a telegram," said Josephine. "I wonder what has happened?"

"Or a dinner-invitation which the servant was told to deliver this morning," I answered. "One would suppose that, after turning out the gas in the hall, one could work without callers."

Having lighted up, and having unbolted the inner door, I beheld, through the glass window of the outer, a young man in a slouch hat. Evidently he was not a telegraph-messenger or a domestic. Nor did he have exactly the aspect of a midnight marauder. Nevertheless, I opened the door merely a crack and inquired, gruffly:

"What do you wish?"

Said a blithe, friendly voice: "I saw your light, and I took the liberty of ringing. Can't you give me three thousand words on the death of the Czar of Russia?"

Before he had finished this sentence, he had backed me, by his persuasive manner, from the vestibule into the hall, and I remembered vaguely that I had seen him somewhere.

"I'm the local correspondent of the New York *Despatch*," he said, to refresh my memory.

I recollected then that he had tried to interview me six months before on my domestic interior, and that I had politely declined the honor. He was a lean, alert, bright-eyed man of thirty-five with a pleasant smile.

"Isn't it rather late to ring my door-bell?" I inquired, with dignity. (My mental language was, "What do you mean, you infernal young reprobate, by ringing my door-bell at this hour of the night on such an impudent errand?" But, in the presence of the press, even a philosopher is disposed to be diplomatic.)

"I needed you, badly," was the reply. "I've got to wire to New York to-night three thousand words on the death of the Czar."

"What do I know about the Czar of Russia?

Why don't you go to the historians or politicians? There are several in the neighborhood. I'm a philosopher."

"I've tried them," he said, with a patient smile. "They were out or in bed. Then I thought of you. Anything you would say on the subject would be read with great interest."

"Pshaw!" I answered.

By this time he had backed me into the dining-room, and, under the influence of diplomacy, I searched for a box of cigars. I had no intention of giving him a single word on the deceased ruler of all the Russias, but I wished to let myself down easy, so to speak, and retain his good-will.

"Ah!" he said, settling in a chair, with a Cabana, "this is the first restful moment I have had to-day." He was pensive during a few puffs, then he added: "A reporter's life is not all strawberry ice-cream. Do you suppose I enjoy rousing a man at this hour of the night? It makes me shiver whenever I do it."

"I should think it might," I answered, in spite of myself. "Some men would be apt to resent it."

"You misunderstand me. I do not shiver from physical fear, but because my sense of propriety is wounded. I dare say," he continued, looking at me narrowly, "that you think I take no interest in the ideal; that you suppose me to be a materialistic Philistine."

You will appreciate that this was startling and especially interesting to me under the circumstances. I, in my turn, examined my visitor more carefully. There were evidences in his countenance of a sensitive soul, and of refined intelligence. The thought occurred to me that here was an opportunity to obtain testimony. "I think that every thoughtful man must take an interest in the ideal," I answered, "and, in spite of the lateness of the hour, I had not set you down as an exception to the rule. Curiously enough, however, I was busy when the bell rang answering a letter from several correspondents in search of the ideal. I will read it to you, if you like, as far as I have got."

Perhaps I hoped that in submitting he would appear slightly crest-fallen. But, on the contrary, he showed obvious enthusiasm at the suggestion, and begged me to fetch my manuscript at once. Josephine met me at the top of the stairs, and whispered that she had been dying with curiosity to know who it was.

"A reporter," I whispered, in reply.

"What does he wish for?"

"Three thousand words on the death of the Czar of Russia," I said, mysteriously; then I picked up my letter and glided away with my finger on my lips. "If he stays too long, dear, you may come down, as a gentle hint."

I began to read, and, as I read, my heart warmed toward my visitor on account of the absorbed attention he paid to my philosophy. "And now," said I, when I had finished, "pray tell what is your ideal? You have told me that you were interested in one."

He shook his head sadly. "No matter about me. It's too late. I can only shiver and go on. But I'm interested in what you're trying to do, and, if you like, I'm willing to throw in a word now and then while you work it out. I'm glad," he added, "that you hit the back numbers a rap."

I told him that he was not exactly intelligible.

"I mean the old familiar aspirants; in particular the lady interested in culture and personal salvation. There was no question about the man of the world and the drummer; one might feel kindly toward them, but of course they must ride second-class, and most newspaper men would ride with them—and some of the editors would have to go third. Easy-going commonness is the curse of democracy, even if I, who am a democrat of the democrats, do say it. But what I like most—and it 's the nub of the whole matter—is that you knew enough to throw out that woman; she might equally well have been a man, for there are plenty of the same sort. If you 'll excuse my saying so," he said, biting his cigar fiercely, "I shouldn't have expected it of a philosopher like you, and I honor your intelligence because of it. The man or woman of to-day in search of the ideal comes plumb up against sweating, bleeding, yearning democracy, and whoever funks, or shirks the situation has no first-class soul—be he or she ever so delicate, or cultured, or learned."

I could not but feel gratified at his fervor, nor did I mind his bringing his hand down on the table with the last word by way of emphasis, for he had grasped my meaning precisely. Evidently, too, he had taken the bit between his teeth and meant to have his say, for, as he lighted another cigar, his nostrils dilated with suppressed earnestness and his eye gleamed significantly.

"I 'm not a man of culture," he continued.

"I have the effrontery, from the necessities of my trade, to ring at your door-bell at midnight, and I know my own limitations, but I know what culture is. When I stand on the cliff and watch the waves hurl themselves against the shore—when on a peaceful summer's night I view the heavens in their glory, I realize in my own behalf something of what those who have had more opportunities than I are able to feel, and I know that I am illiterate and common as compared with many. But, Mr. Philosopher, what has been the philosophy of beauty and art and intellect and elegance through all the centuries until lately? Individual seclusion, appropriation, and arrogance. The admirable soul, the admirable genius, the admirable refinement was that which gloried in its superiority to the rest of the world and claimed the right of aloofness. The monk and the nun lived apart from the common life, and were thought to walk nearer heaven because of it. That idea of the priesthood has nearly passed away, but aloofness and arrogance are still too typical of the mental and the social aristocrats. They glory in their own superiority and delicacy, lift their skirts if they're women, hold their noses if they're men, and thank heaven they are not as the masses are. They are charitable, they are sometimes generous, and invariably didactic, but they hold aloof from the common herd. They refuse to open the gates of sympathy, and sometimes it seems as though the gates will never be opened until they are broken down by the masses."

My visitor suddenly stopped, and started to rise from his chair. Turning to investigate the cause of the interruption, I encountered my wife, Josephine, armed with a tray containing a brazier and the essentials for a midnight repast.

"You will be able to talk better if you have something to eat," she exclaimed, affably.

The ceremony of introduction having been performed successfully without causing our guest to notice that we did not know his name, I begged him to continue his address.

"Yes, do," said Josephine, "while I cook the oysters. I could not help overhearing a little of your conversation, so I know the general drift."
[*Note.*—That means she had been leaning over the banisters, listening.]

"A lunch will taste very good," said the reporter.
[*Note.*—Here he ran up against one of my pet

prejudices, and for a moment I almost forgot that I was doing the honors of my own house. I almost said: "Speaking of democracy and culture, my dear sir, I should like to inquire if you have any authority for your use of the word 'lunch'? As employed by the appropriating and the arrogant it has long meant a meal or a bite between breakfast and dinner; but, as used by democracy, it seems to apply to afternoon tea or late supper equally well."]

"We were speaking of the ideal," he continued, addressing my wife, "and I was just saying that only recently had the world of noblest thought and aims begun to recognize that an ideal life must necessarily include interest in and sympathy for common humanity, and that the mere aristocrat of religion, of culture, or of manners, has ceased to be the Sir Galahad of civilization."

"Indeed it must be so," said Josephine, "and the idea is rapidly gaining ground. People used to be satisfied with making charitable donations; now they investigate facts and conditions and give themselves. But it isn't always easy for those who love beauty to avoid shrinking from people and things not beautiful. There is nothing which freezes a sensitive, artistic nature more quickly than dirt and ugliness, and yet the ideal modern soul does not turn away, but seeks to sympathize and to share. Might you not, dear (Josephine was now addressing me, not the reporter), say that the key-note of the ideal life is refined sympathy?"

"It certainly is an indispensable attribute of it," I answered.

"How much easier it is," mused Josephine, as she stirred the oysters in the melting butter, "to wrap one's self in one's own æsthetic aspirations and to let the common world shift for itself. It was possible, once, to do that and believe one's self a saint, but that day has passed forever. It's very hard, though, sometimes, Mr. Reporter. Constant contact with the common world is liable to make one terribly discouraged unless one has abiding faith in the future of democracy."

"I know it; I know it," he replied, eagerly. "We're a depressing lot—many of us. Don't you suppose I understand how the sensitive soul must suffer when it has to deal with some of us? Take the cheap, ignorant, mercenary, city politician, such as disgraces the aldermanic chair

of our large cities—there's a discouraging monster for you. There is a host of others; the shallow, self-sufficient, impertinent type of shopgirl, whose sole concern is her finery and her
'fellow'; the small dealer of a certain sort, who
adulterates his wares, lies to maintain his cause,
and will not hesitate to burn his stock in order
to obtain the insurance money; the sordid number who seek to break the wills of their relations
who have devised the property to others; the
many, too, who make a mess of marriage, and
leave wife or husband on the paltriest pleas. I
know them well; they are the people, they are
humanity, and they can no longer be ignored
and loftily set aside as 'the uneducated mass'
by those whose finer instincts cause them to live
free from these sins. Hard? Of course it's hard,
but the best hope for the improvement of society lies in the education and enlightenment of
that mass; and this can be compassed only
through the efforts and sympathy of the intelligent and refined."

Just then the clock struck midnight. "Bless
me!" he exclaimed, every one will be in bed,
and what will become of my telegram on the
Czar of Russia? Instead of getting three thou

sand words from you, I have been giving you that number on your own topic."

"For once, then, I have got the better of a reporter," said I.

"But before I give you any supper, Mr. Reporter," said Josephine, "you must acknowledge, too, that the movement *is* gaining ground, and that the refined and educated *are* changing their point of view. Think of the hospitals, think of the museums, think of the colleges, think of the model tenements, the schools for manual training and cooking."

" I do acknowledge it ; it is grand and inspiring. I have been merely calling attention to the fact that in the search for the ideal their new point of view must become permanent and extend still farther. To counterbalance your facts I could cite others. Think of the doings of the multi-millionaires, their modern palaces, their extravagant entertainments, their steam-yachts, their home-desecrating wives—a lot of third-class passengers, with no more claim to be considered first-class than the alderman and the shop-girl and the other democrats of whom we were speaking a moment ago. Nothing of the ideal there, and they had such a grand chance ! Yes, yes, I do

admit, madam, that the efforts and progress of
the refined and intelligent during the last quar-
er of a century have been notable and stirring,
but democracy has been neglected for so many
centuries that it may prove a little ungrateful at
first. And here am I, Mr. Philosopher, keeping
your train in three sections waiting all this time."

" The oysters are cooked," said Josephine.

" Five minutes for lunch !" cried the reporter.
[*Note.*—Confound the man ! Why should he
call my supper a lunch ?]

To *A Young Man or Woman* in Search of the Ideal. IV.

HAT beatific mental condition associated by my midnight visitor, the reporter, with people of alleged cultivation and æsthetic tastes, when in the presence of the beauties or marvels of nature, like sunset, mountain scenery, ocean calm and ocean storm, is doubtless a familiar experience to you. The wonder book of nature is constantly being held up by poet and painter as the source of human ideality, and all the traditions of civilization urge you to attain that degree of artistic development under the white light of which the seals of that book become loosened, and you are able to read in the evening star and the mountain torrent lessons of inspiration and truth. Next to nature in their æsthetic potency are her hand-maids, music, sculpture, letters and painting—briefly, the civilized arts, the medium by which mortals seek to woo and hold fast to beauty. We listen to the gorgeous anthems of the world's most famous composers, and our souls thrill and vibrate with emotion; life seems grand and everything possible. We stand before

the greatest marbles and canvasses, and we seem
to have truth within our grasp and nature almost subjugated. How exquisitely falls on the
senses the sublimity of the lines

> *Fair as a star, when only one*
> *Is shining in the sky.*

We catch a glimpse there of what we call heaven.
Is there any more satisfactory occupation for a
thirsty soul than to scan the fairness of the twi-
light heavens when the evening star shines alone
and the saffron or purple glories of the depart-
ing day irradiate the west?

> *Noi andavam per lo vespero attenti*
> *Oltre, quanto potean gli occhi allungarsi,*
> *Contro i raggi serotini e lucenti.*

So wrote Dante in immortal verse, to portray the
æsthetic value of a kindred experience.

I selected those lines of Wordsworth because
he, of all the poets, suggests more ostensibly in
his verse deliberate pursuit of the ideal. Shelley,
indeed, reveals a bolder purpose to unmask the
infinite, but his mood is oftener that of an audacious stormer of heaven than of a reverent seeker
for perfect truth. We feel in Wordsworth a conscious intent to distill from the study of nature

and of man a spiritual exhalation, which would enlighten him and enable him, by force of his poetic gifts, to enlighten us as to how best to live.
When we think of him, we see him amid the exquisite scenery of his favorite lakes, walking in
close communion with God ; discerning the manifestations of the infinite in the mountain and the
wild flower, in the splendor of the storm and the
faithful doings of the humblest lives.

Ever since he wrote Wordsworth has been
the patron saint of introspective souls. In his
poetry they have found not merely suggestion
but a creed. The poet himself was at heart an enthusiast and a revolutionary, and his worship of
quiet beauty and subjective refinement was the
expression of a design broader and deeper in its
scope than many of his followers have been willing to adopt. He revealed not merely the æsthetic significance of the contemplative life which
substitutes soul analysis, with God in nature as a
guide, for the grosser interests of the flesh, but
also the unholiness of class distinctions and of
the indifference of man to his fellow-man as
distinguished from himself. The followers of
Wordsworth were, for the most part, prompt
to accept the first without including the second

and equally fundamental tenet of his philosophy.
What, a quarter of a century ago, was the ordinary practice of the cultivated and refined, who
had been stirred either directly or indirectly by
the teaching of the great poet to adopt contemplation as the key-note of their daily lives?
Their greatest number was in beautiful, rural
England; but the spiritual atmosphere breathed
by them soon found its way across the Atlantic,
and served to exalt and modify the ever moral
inclinations of New England.

Picture, if you will, the model country house
of the English country gentleman of comfortable means and refined tastes. To begin with,
the structure itself is charming; time has be-
stowed upon it picturesqueness, and art has made
it beautiful with the simple but effective arrange-
ment of vines and flowers. There is nothing of
the vileness of earth at hand to mar or offend.
The proprietor himself, an elder son, has been
left with a competence; no riches, but sufficient
to enable him to pursue his literary or other
refined interests without molestation from pecuniary cares. The interior is tasteful and æstheti-
cally satisfying; the spacious, comfortable rooms
contain all that is desirable in the way of uphol-

stery, ornaments, books, and pictures. The large drawing-room windows command a fair expanse of velvet lawn, flanked by stately trees. Beyond lies an undulating acreage of ancestral metes and bounds, rich in verdure and precious with associations. Here lives our gentleman the greater portion of the year; lives aspiringly according to his Wordsworthian creed. He eschews or uses with admirable moderation the coarser pleasures and vanities of life. Unselfishness, gentleness, and nicety of thought and speech are the custom of his household. He himself finds congenial occupation in literary or scientific research, in the hope of adding some book or monograph to the world's store of art or knowledge. His wife, in co-operation with the church, plays a gracious part among their tenants or among the village sick and poor, teaching her daughters to dispense charity in the form of soup, coals, jellies, and blankets. Parents and children alike, jealously intending to attain holiness and culture, continuously take an account of their individual spiritual successes and failures, and though they hold these auditings with God in the church, they renew them often under the inspiring influence of nature.

The Curfew tolls the knell of parting day,

or, as Dante expressed a similar conception,

'T was now the hour that turneth back desire
In those who sail the sea, and melts the heart
The day they 've said to their sweet friends farewell,
And the new pilgrim penetrates with love;
If he doth hear from far away a bell
That seemeth to deplore the dying day.

This is the hour when the Wordsworthian spirit, refined, conscientious, aspiring, beauty and duty loving, sees through the splendor of the lucent, saffron sky, heaven open, and the angels of God ascending and descending. Not always is the vision so adorable. Often enough the gazer knows the bitterness of divine discontent, and finds the golden glory but a bar, shutting out God. In the favorable hour, though, comes the rapture, and the transfiguration; the exquisite, refined feelings seem to find communion with the infinite, and a voice from heaven to say:

Well done, good and faithful servant.

I have selected this experience of the cultivated English household rather than that of the purely religious life as an example, for the reason that in it the æsthetic side is represented in the soul-hunger, and that the existing conditions of earth are, to a certain extent, taken into account. In the purely religious life, the emotions of the exalted soul have, in the past at least, been prone to exclude the actual conditions of human life from consideration. The thought has been that the earthly existence is travail, and at best a discipline; that the joys of life are vanity, and the mundane problems of life unworthy of the interested attention of the heaven-seeking soul. Modern religious theories have modified this point of view, but certainly in some sects still the æsthetic value of existence is almost contemptuously discarded by religion. I have taken the beautiful lives of the Wordsworthians as an example, also because the religious element is so manifestly cherished and cultivated in them. It is intended in them that art and God should work together, or, more accurately, the precept is that the æsthetic side of humanity is one of the noblest manifestations of the infinite within us. It is significant in this connection that though art has often reached its apogee in periods of moral decay, the ruin of the nation, thus robbed of spiritual vitality, has soon followed, in spite of the glory of its sculpture and canvasses. But that is a mere interjection. The point I wish to suggest is this: The sane soul recognizes, when face to face with truth, that what we see in the glory of the sunset, when we think we walk with God, must be, in order to be of value, an inspiration based on the conditions of mundane life. Without this, prayer and adoration become a mere nervous exhalation, reaching out for something which has no more substance than an *ignus fatuus*. The old saints who lived and died in prayer, ignoring human relations, seem to us to-day to have been wofully deluded. They yearned to be translated from a world to which they had contributed nothing but the desire to be holy. This desire is of the essence of the matter; and so we consent to give their reverences the benison of our distinguished consideration. But aspiring souls, as evidenced by the æsthetic man and woman of culture, presently perceived the error. They recognized that aspiration, to be vital, must start with a conception of the world as it was, and seek a realization of the world as it might be, and that in this seeking lay service to God and preparation for heaven. Proceeding they fixed on unselfish human love and on beauty as the motive of their creed, and endeavored to live lives animated by these principles. This creed has been the real creed of aspiring humanity during the past century and a half, and it still seems sufficient to many. There have been diverse differences of application and administration in connection with it, according as the pendulum swung more or less near to one or the other of the two cardinal points of faith, unselfish love, or exquisite beauty. There have been some who, in their desire to make the relations of man toward those with whom he lived and whom he loved more ideal, have been disposed to ignore the claims of color and elegance; and there have been others so eager in their allegiance to the cause of beauty that they have exalted sense and emotion at the expense of unselfishness and purity. Essentially, however, the ideal life of the modern centuries has sought to develop the individual soul by stimulating its faculties to cherish self-sacrificing devotion to familiar friends, æsthetic appreciation of form, color and sound, and exquisite personal refinement. The Christian life, in its highest form, from this amalgamation of human traits, has constructed an ideal for the soul founded on something tangible and substantial in human consciousness. When the Christian said, "O God, make me pure and noble," it has been no longer necessary to rhapsodize on a heaven concerning which he knew nothing, and to disclaim all interest in this earth. On the contrary, he has appreciated that conceptions of the ideal must be based on human conditions or they cease to be intelligible, and that the soul which seeks God can reach him only through faithfulness to a method of life, the aim of which is to make the best use of earth and its possibilities.

Beautiful as have been the lives which have resulted from this æsthetic spirituality, the world has been beginning to realize, during the last twenty-five years, that this is a creed partially outworn, or, rather, a creed hampered by its limitations. In taking its suggestion for the ideal from the world, noble society chose to accept economic conditions as they were, and to fashion an ideal which necessarily shut out the larger portion of humanity from the possibility of attaining it. The æsthetic satisfaction which we draw from the sunset is due to the pleasure which conscience feels in its allegiance to an ideal of its own devising, and seeing God is only another term for the solemn identification of man's aspirations. The Wordsworthian soul, as interpreted by his followers, assumed that the political conditions of society were always to remain the same, or, more accurately speaking, it accepted those conditions as permanent and continuously inevitable. In other words, it did not foresee democracy. In short, its ideal was essentially aristocratic and exclusive, and it continues so stubbornly in the present day in many circles. To be sure, it has included and continues to include in its formula the carrying of soups, jellies, coals, and blankets to the poor, and the proffering of educational advantages to the ignorant, but it never has predicated, as essential to the world's true progress, such fundamental changes in the social status of society as would involve the annihilation of class distinctions and a greater general happiness for the mass of humanity. To be sure, there have always been individual philanthropists, who insisted upon these changes as vital, but they have been ignored by the leaders of ideal thought as visionary enthusiasts, or maligned as disturbers of permanent society. It has been the struggle of democracy itself that has been the chief revealer of a new vision in the sunset, until now, at last, the soul in search of the ideal appreciates that it does not walk with God unless it sees in the saffron glory its own sympathy with these new conditions.

The development of this recognition has been tolerably swift in certain directions. New hospitals, new colleges, college settlements among the poor, are concrete evidences of the modern spirit, and equally significant, if less heralded, are the faithful, zealous labors of physicians, teachers, clergymen, and the host of workers in various lines of industry, where the earnest, self-sacrificing work done is rarely if ever paid for, in dollars and cents, commensurate with its value. The serious energy of the best humanity, instead of pluming itself in the seductive contemplation of æsthetic beauty, seems rather to be celebrating the apotheosis of dirt. It feels that the cleansing of the physical and moral filth from our slums, the relief of appalling ignorance and superstition, the combating of political dishonesty and the checking of private greed are more to be desired at this time than great marbles and a great literature. Or, rather, perhaps, it seems probable that great marbles and a great literature will not come to us until the leaven of this new ideal expresses itself in the truths of art. The sane, aspiring soul can no longer be satisfied unless it recognizes the inevitableness and the pathos of democracy and adjusts its human perspective accordingly.

The world of vested rights and wealth is still reluctant to accept this new æstheticism, and the soul in search of the ideal will find the allurements of aristocratic culture still insisted on as the secret of noble living. Social arrogance and the exclusive tendencies of class are slow in yielding to the hostility even of republican forms of government. In this country parents who profess to be Americans still choose to send their children to private instead of to the public schools, in order to separate them from the mass of the people. The doctrine of social caste, thus early impressed upon the youth of both sexes, serves to produce a class of citizens who are not really in sympathy with popular government. If one questions sometimes the depth of purpose of highly evolved man, and doubts the existence of God, it is because of the lavish wantonness of living of some of the very rich in the presence of the thousands of miserable and wretched creatures who still degrade our large cities. But there is this to be said in this connection: This new æsthetic ideal is at least partially the fruit of the awakening of humanity to a keener appreciation of the conditions of human life; but its progress is made certain by the coming evolution of democracy, which slowly but surely will overwhelm the aristocratic spirit forever, even though æstheticism, as realized by the arrogant and exclusive, perish in the process. The ideal life to-day is that which maintains the noblest aims of the aspiring past, cherishing unselfishness, purity, courage, truth, joy, existence, fineness of sentiment and æsthetic beauty; but cherishes these in the spirit and for the purposes of a broader humanity than the melting soul has hitherto discerned in the sunset, the ocean, or the starry heavens. There are among us men and women living in this spirit of idealism, and they, O, my correspondents! are the first-class passengers.

To *A Modern Woman* with
Social Ambitions. I.

N the first place let me assure you that I am in sympathy with you. I am not one of those unreasonable philosophers who would have every wife merge her identity in that of her husband, and every spinster who has decided not to marry relegated to obscure lodgings with a parrot and a dog. My sentiments recognize the justice and the value of the emancipation movement by means of which woman has obtained freedom to arrange her life conformably to her own ideas as to what is salutary and entertaining for her as an individual, whether she be married or single, beautiful or plain. In homely phrase the world has become woman's oyster, and, save for the little matter of the ballot, a restriction concerning which the subject-matter of this letter does not require me to agitate you, every woman is at liberty to open her oyster according to her own sweet will. Filial limitations and the other circumstances of her environment must prohibit this and make desirable that manner of living, just as in the case of man; but to all intents and purposes, if she be clear-headed and ambitious, she is free to do what she chooses in the way she chooses, whether it be to preside over a drawing-room exquisitely, to guide a woman's club to grace and glory, to renounce the world for the sake of art and a studio, or, it may be, to combine all these occupations in one seething round of tense existence which, according to the constitution of the subject, is liable to terminate abruptly in nervous prostration or, baffling the predictions of the doctors, to continue indefinitely unto hale and bright-eyed longevity. In brief, I make my best bow to the modern woman; I admire her and am stimulated by her. Indeed, I take her so seriously in her endeavor to be independent that I am almost ready to let her stand up in an electric-car or other overcrowded conveyance. I have on occasions even made so free as to bend forward in the theatre and, lacking an introduction, ask her to take off the high hat which obscured my view of the stage. Verily, these are piping times of progress for woman, as every one knows, and I am glad to put on record as a philosopher that I approve of and am edified by them.

So much, my dear correspondents, to assure

you of my sympathy and my distinguished consideration. There are five of you, but three out of the five—a maid almost hoping always to remain one, a wife almost sorry that she is one, and a widow almost certain that she never will be anything else—have written to me as the result of what is known colloquially as the dumps. That is to say, you have become socially ambitious from stress of circumstances, because your dolls are stuffed with sawdust. But for the letters of Numbers 4 and 5 I should be tempted to adopt the manner of a French philosopher and dismiss you with this piece of counsel: Love some one else. Numbers 4 and 5, respectively, a wife thoroughly happy in the wedded state, and a radiant, able-bodied spinster haughtily unconcerned about love and lovers, are not to be answered by such a simple gallicism. The frame of mind of these two last-mentioned ladies was evidently not induced by disappointment; they are not seeking social activity as an antidote to care or as a mere occupation to consume time. Their letters clearly indicate to me a consciousness of stored-up capabilities and an ambition to display them. Devoted as Number 4 obviously is to

her husband, it is no less clear that she is not
content to be regarded merely as his wife. Similarly, Number 5, though serene at the prospect
of living without a mate, still cherishes the
intention of preserving her identity. In other
words, each is imbued with the desire to make
her individuality felt in the world. It is in the
interest of this justifiable and laudable ambition that I take my pen in hand to compose
an answer. The constituency to which Numbers
4 and 5 belong is large and constantly increasing. There are thousands of women without a
grievance against Cupid whose bosoms are
aching with the desire for identity, and it is
to them, as represented by you, that I address
myself.

Your photographs, furnished as evidence of
good faith in accordance with my requirements,
lie before me as I write. Yours, Number 4 (the
wife thoroughly happy in the wedded state), is
suggestively typical of American womanhood.
I have merely to utilize my mind's eye in order
to behold you in the living flesh, tall, graceful,
spare, and willowy; earnest and piquant in
expression, with an air which suggests both
the desire and the determination to accomplish

great things, including no less a range than the probing of the secrets of the infinite, and the supplying of an ideal domestic dinner. Though willowy still, you have a plumper person than before you were married, and your face has lost the Amazonian tense look which it sometimes wore when you were a maid. Your eyes are bright with happiness, and a shrewd humor plays about the corners of your mouth; humor indicating, perhaps, that you find the world less sorry and more alluring than you did in the days when, grandly aspiring, but a little ignorant, cynical, and severe, you were waiting for an ideal lover to come and lift you from this humdrum, vulgar sphere to the stars. In other words, you have a drawing-room, such as it is, and a baby such as never was, and a husband whose faults (all of which you know) are more than balanced by his virtues, so that you are able to love him devotedly with your eyes open, and thus preserve your self-respect as an intelligent modern, and yet satisfy that primal need of your nature, the capacity for adoring affection. I see you thus in the living flesh, and I see you presently lost in engaging thought. You are saying to yourself some such words as these: "Everything is running smoothly. Alexander's (husband's name) affairs are on a satisfactory financial basis; baby is well, and has cut all her first teeth; the servants seem to be satisfied with us; and now is my chance to do something. What shall it be?"

[*Note.*—"Give an afternoon tea," ejaculated Josephine, to whom I was reading what I had written.]

I have no doubt that my wife is right. That is the first thing you would be likely to do. It is the never-failing resource of the young bride and the aged matron alike when pricked by the spur of social activity. Out go the cards of invitation, thin bread and butter is cut, and presently, on the appointed day, a file or a throng, according to weather and circumstances, of petticoats goes into and from the house, and when the last skirt has disappeared you breathe a sigh of relief and self-congratulation. "Thank heaven, that is over, and I can start afresh with a clear conscience and an erect head." Marvellous are the ways of the modern woman. It is thus that she settles with her social creditors and wins a tranquil soul.

What costs less subtle man canvas-back ducks
and cases of wine is accomplished by the aid
of a few tea-leaves and slices of thin bread and
butter. And then her slate is clear, and she can
afford to sink back for a decade into social
greediness or inactivity, as the case may be,
proud and self-satisfied as a peacock.

Her slate, not yours, Number 4. Mrs. Alexander Sherman let me call you by way of convenience, for a mere number suggests convict
life. As Josephine has intimated, you would probably begin with the tea, but the last visitor
would leave you only temporarily exhilarated.
Within a week carking, though praiseworthy,
care would return, and you would be asking
yourself, "What shall it be next?"

I hear some bluff and old-fashioned man
exclaim, "Let her look after her husband and
children, and attend to her domestic duties."
Do not be concerned by this superficial jibe,
dear madam. I am here to defend you, and I
would be the last person in the world to aid
and abet your aspirations if I were not confident that you are a thoroughly devoted wife
and mother. Let me silence this stuffy censor
at once by informing him that in the interest

of your baby you have familiarized yourself with the laws of hygiene and the latest theories of education, and that in no establishment among your contemporaries of equal means is a better or more punctual dinner served. If I did not believe this to be the case, I would have nothing more to do with you, philosophically speaking.

I am taking for granted, too, that you are not nursing your social ambitions in the same nest with a faith in your own artistic genius. If you believe yourself to be an undiscovered queen of tragedy or an undeveloped poet or sculptor, or feel yourself inspired to write a novel or a play, please consider our correspondence at an end. In such a case, the rest of this letter is not for you. Not because I doubt your genius, but because I am certain that though artistic talent may continue to flourish in spite of a husband and a baby, it must inevitably languish and grow feeble when coupled as a running mate to a career of general, elegant, social usefulness such as I know you aspire to. If you possess artistic genius, or feel that you cannot be happy without testing your own talent in this respect, be satisfied to give one afternoon tea, and then practically renounce social initiative, unless you are prepared to alienate your husband, neglect your baby, or go to an asylum as a victim of triple-distilled nervous prostration. Assuming, then, that you are simply eager to help in working out the problems and fulfilling the destinies of your native civilization with benefit to society and credit to yourself, I see you again in your drawing-room a few days after your preliminary tea, inquiring what you are to do next. I see, too, disporting themselves in your thought, the images of the brilliant women of France of a century ago—such women as Madame de Staël, Madame Récamier, Madame Roland, and others, who influenced affairs of state by their intelligence and social graces. It may be that they have been alike your inspiration and your despair. You would fain follow in their footsteps, but feel a washerwoman as compared with them. Your ambition does you credit, Mrs. Alexander Sherman, and also, begging your pardon, your humble-mindedness. But there is no occasion for you to push either frame of mind to an extreme. Indeed, whether you be a washerwoman or not as compared with these ladies, they were not altogether admirable. I am writing to you as a woman thoroughly happy in the wedded state. You will recollect that of no one of those charming creatures could a similar statement be truthfully made. Madame Récamier's husband was three times her age. He offered, poor man, to consent to a divorce in order to allow his cherished wife to marry another; but she, out of pity for him in his adversity, for he had lost both royal favor and his estate, refused to take advantage of his magnanimity. Madame Roland told her husband, who was some twenty years her senior, her love for Buzot in order to protect herself from herself, and did not allow her feelings an outlet until, every possibility of meeting her lover having been removed by her death-sentence, she could express her passion without violation of duty. Very pretty behavior, but not exactly ideal marital relations, Mrs. Alexander Sherman. They should be taken into account in any comparison which you feel disposed to make between yourself and the ladies in question.

And yet I would not have you fail to appreciate at their full worth the exquisiteness of the heroines of the French salons; the grace and nicety of their manners, the brilliancy of their intelligence, and the thoroughness of their accomplishments. I have given you credit for recurring to them instinctively as models of form, and I should grieve to think that my reference to your superior domestic happiness should lead you to think your humility amiss. Do you know the President of any woman's club who reminds you, by her grace, her nicety, her brilliancy, and her thoroughness of what you imagine Madame de Staël, or Madame Récamier, or Madame Roland to have been? Possibly your patriotism, or even your sincere convictions, would induce you to answer this inquiry in the affirmative; and, indeed, I am ready to admit that we may have their counterparts among us; but certainly the country is not overrun with them, and I have no doubt that so discriminating a person as I imagine you to be will agree that the modern woman is often tempted to seek leadership on the strength of bumptiousness, smart ignorance, and that bustling spirit which those who possess it like to hear described as executive ability, instead of by virtue of the talents and graces of old aristocratic society.

I quite realize, on the other hand, that the conditions under which you live are very different from those which existed when the brilliant and fascinating women whom I have specified, and others resembling them, flourished. They were, of course, the quintessence of civilized society, a small coterie living in the atmosphere of courts, seeking to control events by the force of their engaging personalities. I am writing to you, not as a member of a choice and select organization, from which most women were excluded by reason of their nothingness, but as the representative of a large and growing constituency which is open, in theory at least, if not practically, to the whole world of womanhood. For us, certainly, courts and their atmosphere exist no longer, and the opportunities afforded women by republican institutions to influence the course of political events are slight; but in many respects the outlook of modern woman upon life is essentially broader and no less interesting than the horizon of the mistress of the French salon. Of necessity it is less exclusive and more humanitarian, and by reason of the emancipation of woman as a social factor it includes consideration of the whole range of educational, philanthropic, and æsthetic interests in which democratic civilization is concerned. It seems indeed a long cry from the picturesque experience of a clever and fascinating Madame de Staël, braving the enmity of a Napoleon, or a Madame Roland reading her Tacitus and her Plutarch in the prison of St. Pélagie, to the nervous, bustling, afternoon-tea-frequenting, problem-hunting modern woman of workaday, social proclivities. And yet, I would not have you despair merely because your surroundings lack the color which irradiates their careers. To be different is not necessarily to be inferior. The influence of a noble and beautiful woman may be no less real and no less worthy of emulation in these days of comparatively humdrum world-stage effects and common conditions. But it will be just as well for you, whenever you are tempted to swell with conscious pride and to fancy yourself abnormally illustrious as a consequence—for instance, of being the President of a woman's club, or the triumphant promoter of some reform movement—to stop and whisper to yourself " Madame de Staël," " Madame Récamier."

To *A Modern Woman* with Social Ambitions. II.

*N*OTE.—My wife, Josephine, interposed again at this point. "I have been trying to make up my mind while you were writing," said she, "what she would do next. I mean this Mrs. Alexander Sherman of yours, or whatever her real name is. That is, supposing she had never written to you and sent you her photograph, and she were left to her own devices. I can't blame her exactly for sending the photograph, because you make it a condition of the correspondence; but I can see from her face that she was glad of the opportunity, and that she hopes you will admire it."

"Well, I have," said I.

"Yes, and I agree with you in your enthusiasm. She is handsome, and interesting looking, and ladylike. I was merely considering what she would be apt to do if she had no philosopher to advise her. She has a glad air as you have stated, indicating that she has no domestic or financial grievances, and I don't believe she thinks herself an artistic genius or intends to write a novel. I think, though, that her first tea would elate her a little. She would be glad it was over, but surprised that so many people came. It would set her thinking, and presently she would give a dinner or two and a luncheon or so, and she would go to other teas and dinners and luncheons, and would gradually become the fashion, so that when her friends and acquaintances wished to entertain they would think instinctively of Mr. and Mrs. Alexander Sherman. I am assuming, of course, that her husband is an amiable being and does not thwart her, and is willing to go to a reasonable number of entertainments. She would be punctilious about her calls, and make a point of appearing to remember people, even if she did n't have the least conception who they were, and would be generally blithe, tactful, and gracious. What is the matter, Mr. Philosopher? What would you have her do?" I had said nothing to induce this inquiry, but I suppose I must have writhed involuntarily.

"I dare say it 's all right. I don't see that she could help it; but it sounds conventional," I answered.

"Of course it is conventional; yet, pray,

how is she to avoid conventions? I know you are thinking to yourself that the calls are a waste of time—all men, whether they are philosophers or not, think that. I agree with you that if she were content to shut herself up and be an artistic genius, or merely an everyday wife and mother without social ambitions, she could lead a sane and sufficiently exemplary life without ever owning a visiting card. Remember, though, that this Mrs. Sherman of yours *has* social ambitions, and does not intend to hide her light under a bushel. I assume that she is too sensible to make herself a mere slave to her visiting list, but if you intend to advise her not to call on people who have asked her to dinner, and not to practise the polite observances of civilized society all over the world, I wash my hands of her at the start, and hand her right over to you. Besides, I'm only saying what I think from her face she'd be likely to do. You can give her any instructions you please, and—and we'll see if she follows them."

"I have no doubt it's necessary, if you say so," I answered, meekly. "I shall not venture to offer any radical advice on this point contrary to your judgment. I was merely surmising that the modern woman would find a way to free herself from the manacles of conventional call-paying, which I have heard you yourself declare eat into the flesh and poison the joy of life."

"I have said it in my weary moments," said Josephine, stoutly. "The modern woman uses her common-sense and does not let the manacles hamper her movements; but she knows that she cannot reap social rewards without performing social duties. The modern woman is free, if she sees fit, to disdain social life and all its concomitants and shut herself up in a studio or a college settlement; it is her affair to decide what she wishes to do. But if she decides to be a social promoter and leader, she must continue to call on the people who invite her to dinner, or she is not likely to be asked again."

"I am ready to accept the programme which you have laid out for my correspondent," I replied; "but I should like to know what you mean by social rewards."

"I perceive from your tone, my dear philosopher, that you think I have in mind for your Mrs. Sherman merely a career of social frivolity. Nothing of the kind. I assure you that I appre-

ciate the seriousness of her intention no less
clearly than you do. I desire to help the poor
thing, not to pull her down. I was simply amus-
ing myself by letting her do the things she would
be likely to do if deprived of the benefit of your
wisdom. But you need not be afraid that I underestimate her. Her teas, her dinners, and her
luncheons are merely a stepping-stone toward
higher usefulness. Of course, if she comes to
grief without accomplishing anything, it will be
her fault, not mine. I am giving her her head,
and I trust to her not to lose her mental balance.
Shall I go on?"

"Certainly," said I. "I am all attention."

"She is pretty well known as a social figure
by this time. She has more invitations than she
can accept, and her name appears frequently in
the newspapers as a guest at this and at that entertainment. She is invited to be a patroness of a
series of subscription parties, which flatters her,
and presently to be a patroness of college theatricals, and of a fair in aid of proletarian infants.
It has been her intention to become earnestly
interested in something worthy—the education
of the blind, for instance—and she is trying to
make up her mind what it shall be when she

begins to be deluged with applications to take an interest in all sorts of things, educational, literary, and philanthropic. She receives by the same mail a request to be present at a meeting to promote the moral and hygienic welfare of prisoners, and a notice that she has been elected a Vice-President of the American Mothers' Kindergarten Association. The next day an author asks for the use of her name for a reading to be given 'under the auspices of leading society women.' One evening the servant brings up a card inscribed Miss Madeline Pollard. 'Who is Miss Madeline Pollard?' she asks herself perplexedly. She concludes that it must be one of the educational or philanthropic people she has met of late; then a sudden flush rises to her cheeks, a flush of half-amused, half-indignant excitement. 'Nonsense, it can't be,' she murmurs; then with a stealthy glance at her husband, but without a word to him, she goes down to meet the visitor. She finds a free-spoken and insinuating young woman with an air of pathos. I will give you their conversation, philosopher." (Here is the dialogue as detailed to me by Josephine.)

Visitor. Mrs. Alexander Sherman, I believe?

Mrs. Sherman (with dignity). That is my name.

Visitor. Though we have never met, your person is so familiar to me, that I have taken the liberty of calling. I have admired you at a distance for nearly two years, and I feel sure that you will not refuse me the privilege of knowing you in your home and among your domestic associations. May I sit down?

Mrs. Sherman. Certainly. You have come— er—I don't understand exactly.

Visitor. With your permission to ask you a few questions—to obtain an interview.

Mrs. Sherman (with a manifestation of alarm). You are a reporter? An interview for a newspaper? Oh, I could n't consent on any account. I should n't like anything of the kind at all. You must excuse me.

Visitor (saccharinely). I should not think of publishing anything contrary to your wishes.

Mrs. Sherman. It would be quite impossible. My husband would be very much annoyed. Besides, it would be so ridiculous. I have nothing to say.

Visitor. Mr. Sherman is such a distinguished-looking man. I admire iron-gray hair and mustaches. Indeed, every one would be very much interested in anything you were to say. You are a woman of ideas—a progressive woman. The public is interested in progressive women, and I think such women owe it to the public to let them understand and appreciate them.

Mrs. Sherman. But I'm only a private individual. It might be different if I were an author or other public character; though I don't approve at all of people who parade themselves and their ideas in the newspapers. There! I have hurt your feelings.

Visitor (with her air of pathos). No, dear lady. I'm only a little discouraged. If the public wish to know and progressive people refuse to tell them, what becomes of the reporter who is obliged to furnish copy and to obey orders?

Mrs. Sherman. It is a hard life, I'm sure. But —but, if I'm not impertinent—

Visitor (interrupting). You're going to ask how I came to take it up as a profession. Yes, it is hard; but I glory in it *(proudly).* I'm not ashamed of it. It's a progressive life, too. But it is a little discouraging at times *(sadly).* You have such a lovely home, Mrs. Sherman; elegance without ostentatious display; taste everywhere without extravagance. I should so like to describe it.

Mrs. Sherman. Oh, but you mustn't. Were you ordered to—er—write about me?

Visitor. Yes, dear lady. You are to be one of a series—"Half-hour Chats with our Progressive Women," that's the title.

Mrs. Sherman. Have you—er—been to see any one else?

Visitor. Yes, and they all felt as you did at first *(she enumerates the names of three or four other modern women with social ambitions)*.

Mrs. Sherman. And did they all consent to talk to you?

Visitor. Every one, and they all gave me their photographs.

Mrs. Sherman (faintly). Photographs? You don't mean that you wish a photograph? That would be too dreadful.

Visitor (soothingly). You wouldn't wish to mar the completeness of the series. People like to see those who talk to them.

Mrs. Sherman. But I have nothing to say to them.

Visitor. Leave that to me. You have spoken already. Everything about you speaks—your face, your personal belongings, your household usages. While I have been sitting here I have observed a host of things which talk eloquently of your ideas, your principles, and your tastes. Just the things the public thirst to know about a woman like you. Leave it all to me. I will write it out and send you the proof, and, if it isn't just right, you can alter it to suit yourself *(blithely)*. And the photograph?

Mrs. Sherman. Must I?

Visitor (firmly and boldly). Public people think nothing of that nowadays. It's a matter of course. You would have had a right to feel offended if I had n't included you in my article. You would n't have been pleased, would you now, to see interviews with other progressive women, and your face and personality excluded? Just look at it in that light. It is disagreeable to me to intrude and force my way, and invade privacy, but I have a duty to the public to perform, and from that point of view I count on you to help me.

Mrs. Sherman. Perhaps I ought. Er—would you like it now?

Visitor. If you please.

(Mrs. Sherman goes upstairs and returns presently with a choice of photographs.)

Visitor. They are both exquisite. I choose this one for my article, and, if you don't object, I should like so much to keep the other for myself as a memento of this delightful interview. May I, dear lady?

Mrs. Sherman. If you wish it.

Visitor. Thank you. And there is one thing more. Please write your name on both. An autograph adds so much to the value of a photograph whether it be for the public eye or the album of a friend.

Mrs. Sherman (resignedly). What shall I write?

Visitor. Oh, anything. "Yours faithfully," or "Very cordially yours," are very popular just at present. Thank you so much. And I do hope to meet you soon again. If I should happen to give a little tea at my rooms for Mr. Hartney Collier, the actor, later in the winter, I shall take the liberty of sending you a card. You would like him so much. And now, goodby, dear lady. *Exit.*

I have given this conversation without the various comments and interjections made either by myself or Josephine during the course of it. To have set them forth would merely have

served to mar the sequence of the dialogue.
After announcing the departure of the visitor,
there was a little pause and my wife regarded
me almost pathetically.

"Poor thing!" she murmured, brushing away
the semblance of a tear with her pocket-hand-
kerchief. "I am sorry for her. I can understand
just how it happened."

"For which of the two are you sorry?" I
asked.

"I meant for your woman. But I'm sorry
for them both. It almost seems like fate. The
whole thing is disgusting, but the times are to
blame. The public encourages the reporter and
the interview, and when a woman is told that she
is progressive, and that it is her duty to make
herself felt still more, I can imagine her being
goaded into it if she is the sort of woman your
woman is. I suppose you think I've ruined her. I
did n't mean to; I merely gave her her head, and
that's what she did. I will hand her over to you
now, and you can do what you like with her."

"Excuse me, Josephine. She is your creation.
I should n't think of interfering at this stage.
You have taken her in hand and you must work
out her destiny for her."

"You mean let her work out her own destiny. That's all I was doing. I see your point; and, if you won't take her back, I'm willing to give her her head to the end. I'm interested in her, and I don't despair of her at all, in spite of the fact that you have washed your hands of her. I shall have to think a little before I give her her head again."

Hereupon Josephine assumed an attitude of reflection. When she began to speak presently, her words and manner suggested the demeanor of a trance medium, or seer—as though she were peering into the abyss of the future.

"The interview appears, and her husband is less disturbed than she expects. He declares that the press portrait is an abomination and libellous, but he admits that the text is considerately done for a newspaper interview, and that, barring a few inaccuracies and a little exaggeration due to poetic license, she is made to appear less of a fool than she had a right to expect. This cheers and encourages her, and helps to allay the consciousness that the publication of her face and doings was purely a gratuitous advertisement. She firmly resolves that she will reform and live up to the description of her, and she resolves to devote herself to a more definite field of action. Accordingly, after deliberation, she rejects the case of the blind, and decides to take up the problem of how to make humble homes attractive by simple art. She buys a complete edition of Ruskin, and writes to a half-dozen prominent men and as many women for the use of their names as a nucleus for a club to be known as "The Home Beautifying Society." A meeting is held, and she is elected President and a member of the Executive Committee, facts of which the public is duly informed by her pathetic newspaper admirer. There, philosopher, you see she is doing something serious already."

"You are incorrigible, Josephine," I asserted.

"She means so well, poor dear," my wife continued with a genuinely worried air. "She fully intends to devote herself to that society and make it a success, and she does so for a few weeks. Indeed, she raises money enough to employ a superintendent, and through him to give an exhibition of a poor man's house as it ought to be furnished, and by way of speaking contrast a poor man's house as it is too apt to be furnished when he has money enough to furnish it gaudily. And then she helps get out the annual report, which mentions progress, and shows a balance of $1.42 in the treasury, which leads her to make the announcement that in order to insure the successful continuation of a movement calculated to serve as a potent æsthetic influence among the unenlightened, the liberal contributions made by friends must be renewed in the fall. And then, there are so many other things she has to do. Just listen, philosopher, to what the poor thing has become in less than a year since her life appeared in the newspaper, and tell me what she is to do.

§ 1. Second Vice-President of the American Cremation Society.

§ 2. Member of Text Committee of the Society to Improve the Morals of Persons Undergoing Sentence.

§ 3. Chairman of the Inspecting Committee of the Sterilized Milk Association.

§ 4. Vice-President of the American Mothers' Kindergarten Association.

§ 5. Life member of Society to Protect the Indians.

§ 6. Honorary member of the Press Women's Social and Beneficent Club.

§ 7. Member of the Forty Associates Sewing Bee (luncheon club).

§ 8. Third Vice-President of the Woman's Club, and active participator in the following courses of original work arranged by the members of the Club:

(*a*) Literary Course for 1897–98.
   Shakespeare's Women.
   The Dramatists of the Elizabethan Period.

(*b*) Scientific Course for 1897–98.
   Darwin's Theory of Earth-worms.
   The present Status of the Conflict between
      Science and Religion.
   Recent Polar Expeditions.

(*c*) Political Course for 1897–98.
   The Tariff Bills of American History.
   The Theory of Bimetallism.

§ 9. Member of The Molière Club. (Class to read French plays one evening a fortnight.)

§ 10. President of the Home Beautifying Society. (Her pet interest.)

§ 11. To say nothing of dinner parties, receptions, ladies' luncheons, the opera, concerts, authors' readings, and other more or less engrossing social diversions and distractions.

"There!" continued Josephine. "And this

does not include the thought and worry she spends upon Mrs. J. Webb Johnston."

"And who, pray, is Mrs. J. Webb Johnston?" I asked.

"Her fascinating, deadly, and demoralizing rival," answered Josephine, with a mournful wag of the head. "I am really very sorry, my dear philosopher, that this fresh complication has appeared, for I really think your Mrs. Sherman had all she could attend to already. But I must be faithful to the truth, even though our cherished hopes are thereby frustrated. Must n't I, philosopher?"

"Certainly," said I; "but since you instead of me seem to be writing this letter, I suggest that it is time to give our correspondents time to breathe by beginning a fresh paragraph."

To *A Modern Woman* with Social Ambitions. III.

"JUST as you men—merchants, lawyers, or doctors—" pursued Josephine, reflectively, "deliberately or unconsciously contrast yourselves with your fellows in the same calling and become friendly rivals yet competitors for success and renown, it seems to be inevitable that the modern woman with social ambitions should keep her eye on other modern women with social ambitions and try to make sure that they do not get ahead of her. Your Mrs. Sherman, at the time the newspaper woman visited her, had reached the point where it would naturally occur to her to scan the horizon to observe how the other feminine celebrities of her environment were progressing, and her attention was especially called to the matter by the article on 'Progressive Women.' There she had the opportunity to behold them in their respective glories, and to be jealous of or indifferent to them, according to her judgment as to what each amounted to. It was an interesting list, and she experienced in perusing it, in conjunction with

the portraits, some qualms of mild envy on account of several of the progressionists, but the
only face and career which really discouraged
her were the face and career of the woman I
have referred to, Mrs. J. Webb Johnston, or,
as every one calls her, Mrs. Webb Johnston.

"When she had finished she felt herself essentially on a par with the others; but in the
case of Mrs. Webb Johnston she experienced
a frog in her throat, and she looked into distance with a harassed air for more than five
minutes. Mrs. Webb Johnston was not a stran-
ger to her, but she was comparatively a novelty. That is, she had appeared on the social
stage since Mrs. Sherman herself had become
prominent, and had been making mushroom-
like progress; such rapid progress in fact that
it was only when she read the text of the article that she realized the extent of it. Then it
came over her with a rush that she was in peril
of being distanced on her own ground. For, to
all intents and purposes, they were rivals.
Their visiting lists were practically the same;
they represented and appealed to the same constituency. In personal appearance she could
not justly claim any superiority to Mrs. Webb,

who was at least three years her junior in age,
and who possessed a certain luscious, Juno-like
beauty which was calculated, without question, to
dazzle undiscriminating eyes, and which would
not be regarded except by the very subtle as
inferior in type to her own refined effective-
ness. Yes, there was no doubt about Mrs.
Webb's physical charms, or her great executive
ability, or her enthusiastic devotion to the entire range of interests over which she herself
was aiming to hold undisputed sway. Her own
ambition was to be the guiding spirit, the modern, original social force above all other modern
social forces in her constituency; yet here was
another with an evidently similar ambition, and
a war-cry or shibboleth which was disconcert-
ingly fetching. I trust you have appreciated,
philosopher, that our Mrs. Sherman (I am
really sorry for her now, so I call her 'our'),
from the very first, has been decorously conservative in her point of view, eschewing cheap
and vagabond devices and adhering to elegant
and appropriately conventional usages, such as
seemed to befit a conscientious woman eager
to lead public opinion. If dignified conserva-
tism has been her ruling motive, you will read-

ily appreciate that it would disturb her to find that a Bohemian looseness of social vision distinguished her rival, who had been working her way to the front by the specious cry of 'liberty,' and a seductively expressed intention of freeing the community from the manacles of old fogy conventions. I am sure you will agree, philosopher, that it is natural she should have been worried, or, at least, distracted from settling down to her 'Art in Humble Homes' by this discovery. And investigation and reflection only serve to agitate her still further; for, as the weeks go by, it becomes more and more obvious that the things indicated in the article are true—that Mrs. Webb Johnston is hand in glove with authors, actors, opera-singers, and other celebrities, and that the entertainments which she gives and the conversation heard there lack the dull, cut-and-dried, mechanical flavor observable at ordinary social gatherings. You see the situation, don't you, dear?"

(As Josephine's prophecy has assumed an essay-like or argumentative form, it does not seem to me advisable to interrupt its flow for my correspondents by reciting our side observations, unless they would be material or elu-

cidating. Although her appropriation of my
Mrs. Sherman has proved to be a kidnapping
of a very serious character, and her conversation is bracketed as a " note," still her remarks
seem to me so pertinent that I am prepared to
adopt them as a part of my letter.)

"The most perplexing thing, philosopher, for
a modern woman with social ambitions who
wishes to emulate Madame Récamier or Madame de Staël, is that we have no standards in
this country. Public opinion is the only test of
conduct. The progressive woman is expected
on the one hand to be original, and yet on the
other to guide correctly, and public opinion
reserves the right to follow blindly and to applaud egregiously and afterward to condemn
the leaders whom it has flattered into folly. An
ambitious woman (or a man, for the matter of
that) needs to-day a clear head, a high sense
of responsibility, and a sense of humor if she
or he would avoid being led astray by the will-
o'-the-wisp crew of surface society livers which
pursues talent and originality only to be amused,
and who, provided it is amused, forgives everything else, and eggs the performer on to believe
that its shallow approval is the real verdict of

society. This crew, brought into being by mere wealth, lacking purpose and sneering at it if it threatens to interfere with the progress of the merry-go-round, and backed by the army of society reporters and tittle-tattlers, is a growing factor in our large cities and serves to debauch public sentiment by more and more audacious or frivolous ventures concerning the orthodoxy of which it claims to be the only intelligent judge. We are accustomed to sneer at the formal and confining conventions of older civilizations on the ground that liberty of action is thereby checked and life made artificial, but are we not beginning to discover that there are advantages in a definite prescription as to what gentlemen and ladies can do as compared with a happy-go-lucky system of individual competition in social experiments which, however vulgar and demoralizing, are invariably puffed and glorified by the social gossip editors of a host of newspapers? The subsequent course of Mrs. Sherman's career is an illustration of the plight in which a modern woman with social ambitions is liable to find herself as a result of the democratic habit of constituting the half-educated and often morally obtuse society reporter, her successors and

assigns, the sole arbiter of what is socially elegant and invigorating.

"Setting aside the matter of the ethics of her
egotism, our lady in question is animated by a
conscientious desire to be a refining and admirable influence. It is her ambition to lead, but to
lead nobly and unimpeachably. Her entertainments and her posture in and toward society
have been pursued on this principle, and she has
believed the effect produced by her to be irreproachable intellectual elegance, redeemed from
formalism or dullness by scintillating vivacity.
The suggestion, therefore, that she is behind
the times gives her a genuine shock. She has
hitherto prided herself on her mental acumen
and on her knowingness. She has considered
that she knew life to the dregs, so to speak, for
she had passed through a course of French, and
translated Russian novels, and acquired thereby
a knowledge of things evil, which she kept
stored in her inner consciousness as a source
of pride and an antidote against undue prim-
ness in matters sexual and social. She begins to
ask herself if it can possibly be true that she is
an old fogy, and lacks breadth of view, and that
society in its demands for liberty of conduct and

agreeable entertainment is prepared to discard, as outworn and futile, conventions and limitations which she has been disposed to consider essential to civilized and decent deportment. As the result of this reasoning she resolves to cap her rival's next venture with something of her own. So it happens that not long after Mrs. Webb Johnston has summoned a few select spirits to sup and witness Miss Almira Wing, a visiting coryphée, do a skirt dance, Mrs. Sherman issues notes of invitation to what is mysteriously specified as 'An Eclipse Smoke Talk.' This proves to be a small gathering of choice souls to observe a total eclipse of the moon due at two o'clock in the morning from her own roof, and to listen to remarks by a leading astronomer secured for the occasion. This entertainment is a success, and serves to give her new heart. It was bold, still decent. She has preserved her self-respect, yet shown herself alive to the necessity of being original. She is prompt to reinforce it by an evening with a Russian Nihilist, a young woman reputed to have been prominent in plots to assassinate the Czar, and who makes a specialty of narrating her experiences after a Welsh rabbit, cigarette in mouth.

Naturally, these enterprises spur Mrs. Webb Johnston to fresh efforts of the imagination. Her guests are beguiled at her next evening by a paper on 'Life among the Mormons,' delivered by one of the early female disciples of that community. No men are invited on this occasion. A fortnight later a very small and secretly invited company are bidden to behold an exhibition of the vagaries of a hypnotic patient.

"This enlargement of her horizon, though stimulating, puts Mrs. Sherman on tenterhooks. It becomes necessary for her to keep accurately posted as to the comings of celebrities in order to get the first 'go' at them, so to speak, before they fall into the clutches of her rival. As a consequence, aspirants in every line of art or accomplishment who desire to win the patronage of the public ask for the use of her name and receive it. She had been nervous and over-occupied before, but now her days are passed in a ferment. She has recourse to tonics and to sleeping draughts. She feels elated at the success of her enfranchisement, but a feverish interest as to what Mrs. Webb Johnston will do next keeps her uneasy. Nor has she forgotten her serious intentions. She tries to assure her-

self that her progressiveness is for the benefit
of society, and that she is leading it in noble directions. She still retains her scruples. She draws
the line on women celebrities of unchaste life. In
this she refuses to be led astray by her rival's
practices. Mrs. Webb Johnston's openly avowed
theory had been that where art was concerned,
she chose to ask no questions. Accordingly, she
took to her bosom, socially, any one who was
brilliant or attractive; and every notoriously erot-
ic actress, singer, dancer, or other artist whose
talent had caught the public fancy was invited
to her house, and became privileged on very
short acquaintance to kiss her and call her by
her first name.

"Mrs. Sherman's conscience obliges her to
draw this line, but she is conscious that it is an
inconvenience to do so, which puts her at a dis-
advantage. Mrs. Webb Johnston has merely to
swoop down on the hotel, or insinuate herself
behind the scenes, and offer her visiting card,
and presently her cheek, in order to carry off
the prize. She cannot but feel that there are advantages in the Bohemian democratic point of
view which asks no questions, but takes the good
without heeding the ill.

"By refusing social recognition to women whose private characters are disreputable, she is shutting herself off from alluring friendships with sopranos, contraltos, tragediennes, skirt-dancers, music-hall singers, and many other brilliant and fascinating creatures whose presence at her house could not fail to make her entertainments interesting to her guests. All these women are sought out and cherished by Mrs. Webb Johnston.

"The old adage that there are other ways of killing a cat than choking her with cream, comes pertinently to mind in this connection. Conscience is apt to be a tyrant if deliberately overridden, but it may be hoodwinked with comparative complacency. Mrs. Sherman remains true to her principle of excluding meretricious characters from social intercourse with her guests, but she reserves to herself the right of passing on the evidence. Seeing that she had read Madame Bovary and Anna Karénina, was she not amply qualified to detect immorality at first blush? That seemed to be almost an essential attribute of a modern woman with social ambitions.

"The occasion for putting into practice this

prerogative was not far to seek. The arrival from
Europe of one of the most brilliant of the galaxy of foreign actresses brings her heart into her
mouth. She reads eagerly everything which the
newspapers have to say about her, and naturally
finds nothing there suggestive of impropriety.
She buys and scans photographs, and these
merely serve to heighten the ideal estimate
which has shaped itself in her mind. She refuses to entertain sundry rumors which have
reached her to the effect that the lady in question has been successively maintained by a
French marquis, and a Russian banker, and was
at present reputed to be on unduly intimate
terms with the famous leading man of her own
troupe. To the person who has confided to her
these whisperings she answers, 'I don't believe
a word of it,' and then adds, significantly, 'Wait.'
The person is a man, and he shrugs his shoulders. But her soul is jubilant in its faith and in
the hope that at last she has found a way to compete with Mrs. Webb Johnston.

"On the day when the actress arrives in town
Mrs. Sherman goes to see her. The meeting is
by appointment at ten o'clock in the morning,
and lasts more than two hours. They come down-

stairs together with the mien of happy sisters. Mrs. Sherman's face wears a seraphic smile. Her carriage is in waiting, and in it they are driven to her home for luncheon, and on the same evening cards are issued for an after-theatre supper-party as a preliminary announcement of impending festivities. She sends for the man who told her the rumors, and in a triumphant tone says, 'My friend, your stories are untrue; I have been to headquarters. I have seen her and asked her, and she has assured me, with tears in her eyes, that they are a wicked falsehood—a malicious, baseless slander.'

" 'Surely,' says the man, 'she ought to know,' and then he shrugs his shoulders again, a caustic act which, though done as a friend, provokes Mrs. Sherman to anger, and puts a chasm between them.

"On this day the cat is killed, and yet the cream is saved. True to her principles, Mrs. Sherman still bars her doors against the wanton, yet never fails to convince herself that she is an infallible judge of virtue. If there are rumors and whisperings in advance, she invariably takes the bull, or, more accurately speaking, the heifer, by the horns and puts the inquiry. The answer settles the matter. It becomes a veritable 'open sesame' to her entertainments and her friendship. She shows herself in public with her arm, metaphorically and literally, around the waist of women whom all men know to be unchaste and living in violation of social laws. They kiss and talk poetry and art and philosophy, and her face gleams with the consciousness of new importance and the realization of her ambition.

"Mrs. Sherman has now reached the point where she feels that she can fairly regard herself as the most busily progressive woman of her community. She has a finger in every pie, literary, artistic, philanthropic, educational, and what not. She is always in a hurry, and she does nothing thoroughly. Her ideas jostle against each other in their promiscuity, and become all jumbled together in her consciousness. Her time is so occupied that when she is doing one thing and talking to one person, some other thing or person is in her mind, though her social skill often enables her to conceal the fact. Her life is one continuous series of kaleidoscopic sensations and emotions without system or result. She is ostensibly a leader, but her leadership suggests only ceaseless activity and indiscriminate, super-

ficial posings and vanities. Her nerves are kept
in a constant state of tension by breathless comings and goings, her digestion perpetually tried
by the viands of festivities. Nor is her conscience
satisfied. A vague unrest pursues her still, tor-
turing her by insinuations of her own utter fu-
tility, yet goading her on to fresh efforts. She
presently becomes a wreck morally, mentally,
and physically, though she preserves a bold front
to the world, until one day the news is flashed
upon a busy public that she has died suddenly
from 'heart failure' following an attack of pneu-
monia. The physician in attendance shakes his
head when asked to give assurance of her recov-
ery. He possesses an instinctive knowledge that
she has kept her vitality keyed up to concert
pitch by antipyrine, phenacetine, and the other
drugs to the use of which modern progressive
women are addicted. And so no more of Mrs.
Alexander Sherman.

"Of course," continued Josephine, "it was
not strictly necessary to kill her. The constitu-
tions of some progressive women seem to be
proof against anything. But the chances were in
favor of her death. And if the poor thing had
lived, what hope was there for anything but a

vapid old age, haunted by visions of her decreasing notoriety? And the strangest part of all is that when I began with her I felt hopeful that she would amount to something. The laws of evolution are not to be trifled with, however, even by the wives of philosophers."

To *A Modern Woman* with Social Ambitions. IV.

I FEEL confident that my correspondent, Number 4, a wife thoroughly happy in the wedded state, will appreciate that there was nothing personal in Josephine's portrayal of Mrs. Alexander Sherman's career. It seems to me that it presents, more clearly than any arguments or words of mine could do, the perils of egotism and superficiality, and that I need not further indicate to my correspondents that to do a little of everything and nothing thoroughly, to be so eager for individuality or notoriety that one is ready to be led instead of to lead, and to discard social canons on the plea of liberty or superior feminine acuteness, will produce a nervous, emotional, gibbering type of character adapted to cause Madame de Staël or Madame Récamier to turn in her grave. Neither you, Number 4, nor Number 5, the radiant, able-bodied spinster, haughtily unconcerned about love and lovers, need fear any detriment to your souls or to your social progress as a consequence of doing some one or two things well, and of refusing to sacri-

fice your self-respect to the urgency of cheap substitutes for refinement and elegance. Certainly,
thoroughness and delicacy of thought and sentiment are essential to the modern woman who
would be socially effective in the best sense.

Let me here state that I am entirely conscious
that it is not a prerequisite to earnest living to
be socially effective at all. One can pursue one's
occupation, be it house-keeping, school teaching,
scientific philanthropy, or novel writing without
taking any part in what is known as society, and
still be respectable and worthy in character. Yet
if every woman were simply to eat her three
meals a day, sleep, be affectionate to her family,
reasonably charitable, and do her daily task, the
world would lose much of its vivacity, color,
and æsthetic interest. As the world is at present
constituted the greater mass of human beings,
both male and female, are shut off from participation in society in its narrower sense. Their
means, their manner of living, and their tastes
confine them to very simple or else to very
coarse social diversions. Hence we are accustomed to read in the newspapers of "society
people," as a term of reproach indicating that
portion of the population which cultivates the

social or æsthetic side of nature in its leisure hours. The demagogic force of the term is derived from the undeniable existence of a surface element of society, which has been and is still apt to conduct itself in such a manner as to subject itself justly to the charge of frivolity and extravagance. But the unthinking extend its application to the cultivated and intelligent many, who in all countries constitute the best force of the community. Society in this better sense must always exist, and, although the woman who holds herself aloof from it may not be distinctly culpable, there can be no question that those who succeed in participating in the social interests open to them, without neglecting or allowing them to obscure sterner pursuits, live finer and more serviceable lives than those who pass all their hours of relaxation by the chimney-corner, either because they fancy that essential to comfort or because they choose to despise what they call, with a virtuous inflection, "society."

This may sound elementary, but I present it as a premise to what is to follow. You, my correspondents, are ambitious to progress socially, yet doubtless you are not altogether impervious to the seductive suggestion that social interests

are hollow and unprofitable. For instance, I feel
sure that you, Number 5, the radiant, able-bodied spinster, haughtily unconcerned about love
and lovers, feels the pressure of the times, and
would regard the life of a Madame de Staël or a
Madame Récamier, however brilliant or picturesque, as at variance with modern theories of social utility. I hear you making some such repre-
sentation as this, which is merely an enlargement
of the letter you wrote me: "Here am I, a young
woman of some means, without family responsibilities or other demands upon my time. I
have no prejudice against marriage; indeed, I
earnestly hope to meet some day, some man
who will love me and whom I may love, and
whose wife I may become; but as I am no
longer so young as I was once, being nearly
thirty, I have no intention of bothering my
head about the subject further, and so put it
aside as a contingency. I have no special talent;
that is, I never could accomplish anything unusual with my voice, my pen, or a brush. I
have taken, and I do take, a strong interest in
charitable enterprise and investigation. I belong
to philanthropic societies, and it has more than
once occurred to me to join a college settlement

and live among the poor. I have friends who do that; but I do not feel a special fitness for the work. Nor am I sure that, however valuable that experience may be as a form of loving service to the people one hopes to influence, it • can be other than episodic and limited to the individuals who are conscious of the need or of the inspiration. I am painfully aware of the dissipations and vanities of fashionable people, in many of which I have taken part myself, and have no desire to be merely a frivolous devotee of social amusements. And yet I feel sure that the social side is no less genuine in its claims upon us than any other. It seems to me that I might interest myself socially, but I am puzzled by the intricacies of the situation. It is so difficult to be democratic in one's sympathies and yet maintain the old standards of elegance and refinement. To be socially effective one ought to be in touch with modern social tendencies and yet be true to the finest instincts of aspiring womanhood. What can one do to realize this?"

That is, I believe, a clear presentation of your state of mind and its dilemma. Having read of the vicissitudes of Mrs. Alexander Sherman, you have probably a more distinct idea of what

you ought not to do; but would have a right to
argue that a mere warning loses half its force
unless a substitute be supplied. To begin with,
you are correct in your assumption—you see I
credit you with a considerable intelligence—that
if you hope to be effective you must not be content with mere aristocratic elegance. That is a
requisite which will gain you a standing within
certain narrow limits, and if cleverly cherished,
may bring you a surface reputation which the
society newspapers will vie with each other to
enhance. The acquirement of mere fine ladyism
is going on actively in our society, and though
it has not turned the heads of so many American women as its opposite, superficial democratic smartness, it seems too apt to fill the
breasts of its votaries with a pleasing self-satis-
faction, which no suggestion that the gift is not
original serves to disturb. It is a product of and
inheritance from the older civilizations, and in
its most precious but not its exaggerated form,
is absolutely essential to the most highly evolved
womanhood. A fringe of our people in the North
and in the South, and latterly in the West, has
always insisted on and cultivated it, generally
with much credit, and has thereby evoked the

taunt that they were out of sympathy with the institutions of the country. That has been far less true than demagogues would have us believe, but there has been enough truth in it, and there is still enough truth in it to put our well-bred class—"society people," as they are called —on their guard against themselves. There is certainly nothing essentially American in conventional fine manners and in the conventional social tone which people of breeding the world over cultivate, and where these are the possessor's chief or only title to superiority, and are worn as such, there is room for the sneer that he or she is not an American at heart.

During the last twenty years our population has been passing through a period of awakening in regard to the usages of civilized countries, with the result that the public point of view has been astonishingly readjusted. The people are, so to speak, tumbling over each other in their haste to adopt Old World social customs, and the paragrapher who tells us that the wife of the Chief Magistrate wears blue novelty silk waists to the theatre, made by one of her familiar friends, makes a point of assuring us that the dressmaker in question is herself "a leading society woman." Our public press is rife with society cant and society gossip, and justifies the practice on the plea that the plain people are absorbed in the contemplation of the doings and the dresses of those whom they know only by hearsay, even as an Englishwoman will run the risk of apoplexy in order to catch a passing glimpse of her sovereign. Of this appetite for social tittle-tattle, the wealthy class seems disposed to take every advantage, pluming itself on its new importance to the point where it is constantly trying to devise some new extravagance or inanity.

But this is not the spirit of the United States, nor are these the best Americans. Our nation is strange in this respect. We wear our faults upon our sleeves, or rather we suffer a surface population to belie us in various walks of life. That is the reason why the foreigners who come over here and try to amass the materials for a book in a few months fail to understand us as we really are. They are led by superficially prominent indications to believe many things which are true only of a limited portion of the population, and they fail to perceive the sturdiness of character, the independence of view, and the social charm which distinguishes a large and constantly increasing portion of the American people, who are neither extravagant plutocrats nor vulgar republican braggarts and despisers of civilized practices.

During the early years of our history as an independent nation, the imitators of foreign and civilized usages, the well-bred people of our country were, as I have indicated, regarded as out of sympathy with the population at large, and there was a certain justification in the charge; for though there was no conscious slur on the part of these students of manners, they were at fault in that they failed to manifest or to take an interest in that energy, originality, and freshness of mental vision which was known as Americanism. Blatant and mortifying as this national tendency was in its exaggerated forms, it was a genuine indigenous product typical of the native character. Chastened and subdued in New England, and assuming outrageous expression on the prairies, it was the real manifestation of our entity as a new departure from the peoples of Europe. Hence it was natural that those who were shocked by or felt no kinship for this trick of the blood should be looked at askance. Among those who claimed in their own hearts social prestige it was long the fashion to shrug their shoulders over the raw eccentricities of their fellow-countrymen, which, as revealed both in public affairs and during European travel, were often startling to precise taste and wofully suggestive of the boaster. Yet those very traits in their truer expression have been the vital force of the people, and give us our savor as a nation. Not to possess them is to be without the characteristics of an American.

The experience and events of fifty years have served to soften the eccentricities and tone down the unconventional manifestations of the national spirit. Although the prairies and the halls of Congress still afford occasional rampant types, the great body of the people is eager, as I have indicated, to adopt cosmopolitan usages. But the salt of the native character remains undiluted in the blood of the people, and marks them as genuinely as ever, though they have learned to avoid some of the exuberance of language and look which made foreigners smile, and their sensitive countrymen blush when they met them in the picture galleries of Europe.

Most significant among the changes which experience and time have brought to pass has been the development on the educational and social side. Always alive to the importance of general education, but unfortunately so proud of the maintenance of public schools that it was disposed to sneer at any learning not to be acquired at them, the American people—that portion of it which foreigners are so apt to overlook when they attempt to charaĉterize us—is seeking to foster in a variety of ways the opportunities for higher learning, and wider intelleĉtual intelligence. Within the last twenty-five years not merely an array of colleges and other educational institutions have sprung into existence, but with them an army of disciples whose clubs and classes and associations for the investigation and study of all the forms of learning from English literature to Sanscrit have given a new tone and stimulus to the social side of American life. An independent, but now generally respeĉtful eagerness to learn has taken the place of an independent ignorance relying upon its own infallibility, which was often worn as a chip upon the shoulder. With it all has been manifest the same originality, independence, and energy of spirit which has been conspicuous from the first. This still serves to handicap as well as to promote progress, for it is apt to beget undue self-confidence and lead our new women and eager youth of both sexes to ignore the accumulated wisdom of older civilizations, and claim a special clearness of vision, the only basis for which is often half-digested superficial knowledge. But educational and professional life all over the country is being constantly enriched by more and more competent students and practitioners who stand not merely for what is best and most earnest in American life, but who typify the true American spirit. While the omniscient class in the population has become less assertive and more humble-minded, the class which was once politically proscribed in some sections of the country because it was cultivated and because it shrugged its shoulders in spite of its breeding, has undergone a transformation also. A large portion of it, always patriotic at heart so far as dying was concerned, has learned to recognize that it must live in sympathy with our republican institutions if it would not be regarded as an exotic, and that aloofness is akin to lack of patriotism. A fringe of vain and more and more extravagant and self-indulgent society exists in our large cities, especially in New York, which affects to claim social superiority to the rest of the population, and is indifferent to national progress and to the best public interests; but it is numerically small, and, except in the newspapers, a very unimportant factor of influence as compared with the already large and growing body of citizens over the country which is eager to live nobly and wisely. This right-minded and aspiring class represents the drawing together and amalgamation of the once seemingly hostile poles of opinion typified by the conservative, civilized, sedate, social aristocrats of the nation, and the independent, assertive, ignorant but truth-seeking sons and daughters of the soil. Each has recognized the justice of the other's criticisms, and as the outcome of a mutually amended point of view we have an earnest, intelligent, and interesting alliance, which insists on both fineness and strength of fibre as essential to progressive national character. The confines of this belt of good citizenship shade away into stiff or heartless conventionalism on the one side, and smart, obtuse, social perceptions on the other, but it is constantly widening and undergoing the refining process which results from the increasing intelligence of the contracting parties. By way of exemplification in matters feminine may be instanced the more and more frequent requirement by those in authority in women's colleges that applicants for the position of teacher should possess those evidences of gentle nurture which the world is accustomed to associate with the word "lady." Conversely one may point to the fact that originality, independence, and suggestiveness are no longer repulsed by the conservative, but welcomed as a leavening grace necessary to the development of a finer womanhood.

To the existence of this alliance I would call the attention of the modern woman with social ambitions—you, in particular, Numbers 4 and 5. For it seems to me that in its perpetuation and extension lies the best hope of society. It represents, of course, an involuntary approximation of contrary opinions, and has no definite corporate existence, like a woman's club, for instance. But the alliance is real, nevertheless, whether it be deliberate or not. Certainly the American woman who wishes to lead effectively and aspiringly can no longer be either of the insipidly fashionable or the smart, assertive, schoolma'am type. In her composition that eager, star-investigating spirit, which through all the phases of her brilliant but often nerve-harrowing evolution has distinguished her, must curb itself to the yoke of social refinement. On the other hand, the day has passed when the charms of mere convention, of graceful elegance fortified by nothing deeper than wit, or supple-ness of mind, would rank the possessor among the leaders of society.

Imitation, therefore, of the witchery worn by the women of the French salons will, however successful, if it be limited to mere manners and mental accomplishments—the pyrotechnics of social adroitness—gain for the modern woman of ambition, be she discerning and honest with herself, only a sore conscience. First of all, let her be a lady—elegant, gracious, pure, and tender; but, last of all, let her be merely that and stop there, looking down with amiable supercilious-ness on the world outside the narrow limit hedged by the conventions of those who play at living, and fancy themselves the real world. It is becoming more and more easy in this coun-try to be a fashionable fine lady, without audible reproach, for the class of mere society people is a growing one. Yet to those who are content thus to waste their lives, the difficulty of being recognized as anything but society persons is just as great as ever, for though the ranks of the alliance may seem to terminate on one side in their direction, there is a dividing chasm between them broad as is the difference between careless aristocracy and sympathizing humanity. On one side of this chasm live those whose vital interest is to be exquisite and to be entertained; on the other, those whose souls are bent upon the finest aspirations and hopes of the race. In the heart of this alliance between conventional culture and humanity the reforms, the enterprises, and the safeguards projected for the advancement of modern society are born, and here they find their truest champions.

It is not easy, however, my correspondents, to decide whether there lies greater danger for the modern woman with social ambitions in the allurements of mere fashionable society, or in the temptations to be smart, superficial, and common, which confront her at the point where the alliance shades toward the camp of democratic individuality. Here there is a second chasm; yet, like the sunken road into which the cuirassiers of Napoleon fell at Waterloo, it is not evident at first glance to those who, fired by the ardor of youth, but socially unenlightened, tilt at fame and world progress. The evolution of democracy having in the case of woman been supplemented by the enfranchisement of her sex, present conditions afford extraordinary opportunities for the exercise of her new-found liberty. So secure is her position, so welcome is her announced determination to readjust and regenerate the world, that humanity is prepared to give her her head and to applaud every sign of advancement.

But man, though thus encouraging and at heart keenly appreciative, is watching her closely, and there can be no question that if he has to choose between the old-time woman of convention—the exquisite, picturesque doll of society—and a monster who revolts at sex, sneers at sentiment, and administers the affairs of life on a dull, utilitarian basis enlivened only by knowing, mundane humor, he will prefer the doll, or, if she be out of the question, he will fight the monster. It would be St. George and the dragon again! Long has the idea which the poet put into words,

Man's love is of man's life a thing apart,
'T is woman's whole existence,

[121]

been uttered with a sigh by our wives and mothers; yet with pride, too, and a secret joy in
spite of the melancholy inflection. There are
some women to-day who would throw off the
yoke of this adage and enter the lists of life on
the footing of a second-class man, proud of their
swagger, and with the instincts of the wife and
mother sternly repressed. Fortunately, to the
woman of the alliance this new woman of democratic individuality is as abhorrent as she is to
men. But it is not in her extreme type that she
is as yet most dangerous, for admiration comes
only by degrees. The danger lies in the failure
to recognize the species in the bustling, chirp-
ing, metallic, superficial class of women which
in some numbers, and with the wiry whirr of
grasshoppers, infests the cities and towns of the
republic to-day—women who have no reverence and no sentiment, no desire to learn for the
sake of knowledge, but merely for ostentation
—women who have not progressed as souls, but
who have substituted coarseness for aspiration,
and material "cuteness" for unsophisticated
purity of thought and sentiment.

The modern woman with social ambitions
must be essentially a modern woman. That is,

she must recognize the justice of and sympathize with the aspirations of society for a broader humanity, and she must recognize and be a party to the responsibilities placed upon her own sex by the process of emancipation. Now, if ever, is the opportunity for woman to show what she is made of. If she is made simply of sugar and spice and all that is nice, as we are informed in the nursery rhyme, we shall have to accept her as she is, and put up with her delightful volatility and tender but unintellectual limitations. If, on the other hand, as the world is ready to believe, she is a star-seeking creature, who has been kept down, she will soon be able to give manifest signs of her ability to soar; and it is equitable to remind her that the burden of proof is on her. She cannot afford, distinctly, to be superficial. She must be thorough both in her investigations and her intuitions or she will amount to nothing, for it must be remembered that though man may be slow at intuition, he is capable in investigation. Every woman of the present day who becomes either an elegant voluptuary or an egotistical, metallic flibbertigibbet, furnishes one more piece of evidence for the edification of those who maintain that the men-

tal constitution of her sex, save in its capacity
for affection, is shallow. That is probably not
the truth, but she should make the demonstra-
tion of the calumny more complete. Woman's
authority over matters social is far greater than
it has ever been. Not only as regards the social
manifestations of society, but in the matter of
the deeper problems of social living upon which
the progress of society depends, her influence is
becoming more and more a vital factor and force.
If she is sincere, society will become both more
earnest and more attractive; if she is simply seeking liberty at the expense of religion, purity,
sentiment, and the fine things of the spirit, it
were almost better she were again a credulous,
beautiful doll, and remained so to the end of
time. Clearly, the modern woman with social
ambitions must not neglect to hold fast to the
old and everlasting truths of life in her struggle
toward the stars. Sympathy with and capacity to
promote new ideas are essential to her progress,
but only by allegiance to the eternal feminine,
to the behests of love and motherhood and
beauty of imagination, can the development of
society on the lines of a broader and wiser humanity be effectually established.

To *A Young Man* wishing to be an American. I.

I WROTE this once as a definition of Americanism: "It seems to me to be, first of all, a consciousness of unfettered individuality coupled with a determination to make the most of self." In short, a compound of independence and energy. To you, in the earnest temper of mind which your letter of inquiry suggests, this definition may seem a generality of not much practical value; declarative of essential truth, yet only vaguely helpful to the individual. Yet I offer it as a starting-point of doctrine, for to my thinking the people of the United States who have impressed themselves most notably on the world have possessed these two traits, independence and energy, in marked degree. And to you, whatever your condition in life, if you consider, it must be apparent that manly self-respect and enterprising force are essential to character and good citizenship, and that the prominence accorded to these qualities by those who have analyzed the component parts of our nationality is a dis-

tinction which should be perpetuated and rein-
forced by succeeding generations.

Nevertheless, the counsel seems to approximate a glittering generality for the reason that
the opportunities for acting upon it no longer
sprout on every bush as in the forties, fifties,
sixties, and seventies of the present century when
we were a budding nation and much of our territory was still virgin soil. I write "seems to
approximate" advisedly, for the opportunities
are just as plenty, merely less obvious. Yet here
again I must make this qualification—one which
recalls doubtless the favorite aphorism employed
to meet the plea that the legal profession is
overcrowded—that there is always an abundance
of room on the top benches. Indisputably the
day has passed when the ambitious and enterprising American youth could have fruit from
the tree of material fortune almost by stretching
out his hand. Now he has to climb far, and the
process is likely to be slow and discouraging.
The conditions peculiar to a sparse population
in a new country rich in resources have almost
ceased to exist, and, though a young nation still,
we are face to face with the problems which concern a seething civilization where almost every

calling seems full. Now and again some lucky seeker for fortune still finds it in a brief twelvemonth, but for the mass of American young men the opportunities for speedy, dazzling prosperity have ceased to exist. Those who win the prizes of life among us nowadays owe their success, in all but sporadic cases, to unusual talents, tireless zeal and unremitting labor, almost as in England, and France, and Germany. So also, with the passing of the period when enterprise and ambition were whetted by the promise of sudden and vast rewards, have disappeared many of the traits, both external and psychological, which were characteristic of our early nationality. The buffalo is nearly extinct, and with him is vanishing much of the bluff, graceless assertiveness of demeanor which was once deemed essential by most citizens to the display of native independence. Our point of view has changed, broadened, evolved in so many ways that it were futile to do more than indicate by a general description what is so obvious. Partly by the engrafting and adoption of foreign ideas and customs, partly by the growth among us of new conditions beyond the simple ken of our forefathers, our national life has become both complex and cosmopolitan. If we, who were once prone to believe our knowledge, our manners, and our customs to be all-sufficient, have been borrowing from others, so we in our turn have been imitated by the older nations of Europe, and the result is an approximation in sympathies and a blurring of distinctions. Political differences and race superficialities of expression seem a larger barrier than they really are, for in its broader faiths and vision the civilized world is becoming homogeneous. The ocean cable and the facilities for travel have palsied insular prejudice and lifted the embargo on the free interchange of ideas. The educated American sees no resemblance to himself in the caricatures of twenty-five years ago, and rejoices in the consciousness that the best men the world over are essentially alike. This, perhaps, is only another way of reasserting that human nature is always human nature, but this old apothegm has a clearer significance to-day than ever before.

Yet the opportunities for the display of enterprise and independence remain none the less distinct because we are becoming a cosmopolitan community and the old spectacular flavor has been kneaded out of the national life. Much of our free soil has been appropriated by an army of emigrants from Europe, and in connec-tion with this fact the saying is rife that every foreigner seems infused with a new dignity from the moment that he becomes an American. This may be bathos in individual cases, yet it is the offspring of truth. Still it remains equally true that we have an enormous foreign popula-tion whose ideas and standards are those which they brought with them. Proud as these men and women may be of their new nationality, and eager as they may be to aid in the promotion of good citizenship, their very existence here in large numbers has altered the conditions of the problem of Americanism. The problem involved is no longer that of the winning of a new land by a free, spirited people under a republican form of government, but the larger equation of the evolution of the human race. Americanism to-day stands in a sense more accurate than be-fore as the experiment of government of the people, for the people, and by the people, and for the most complete amalgamation of the blood of Christendom which the human race has ever known. We have lately been celebrat-ing our centennial anniversaries. Already the great figures of our early history seem remote. The struggle in which we are engaged is intenser and broader than theirs: It concerns the progress of human society. You, whom I am addressing, find yourself a unit in a vast, heterogeneous population and a complex civilization. You live in the midst of the most modern aspirations and appliances, and cheek by jowl with the joy and sorrow, the comfort and distress, the virtue and vice of a great democracy. Your birthright of independence and energy finds itself facing essentially the same perplexities as those which confront the inhabitants of other civilizations where the tide of existence runs strong and exuberant. If our nationality is to be of value to the world, Americanism must stand henceforth for a rectification of old theories concerning, and an application of fresh vitality to the entire problem of human living.

Love of country should be a part of the creed both of him who counsels and him who listens, yet I deem it my duty, considering the nature of our topic, to suggest that there are not a few in the world, foreigners chiefly, who would be disposed to answer your inquiry how best to be an American, by citing *Punch's* advice to persons about to marry, "don't!" It does credit to your love of country that you have assumed a true American to be a consummation devoutly to be emulated. Humility on this subject has certainly never been a national trait, and I cannot subscribe to any such doubt myself. But yet again let me indicate that across the water the point is at lest mooted whether the seeker for perfect truth would not be nearer success if incarnated under almost any other civilized name. Let me hasten to add that I believe this to be due to national prejudice, envy, and lack of intelligent discrimination, especially the latter, in that the foreigner is mistaken as to the identity of the true American. It behooves you therefore to ascertain carefully who the true American is, for even my defence seems to hint at the suggestion that all Americans are not equally admirable. Forty years ago an intimation that all Americans were not the moral and intellectual, to say nothing of the physical, superiors of any Englishman, Frenchman, German or Italian alive would have subjected a writer to beetling criticism; but, as I have already intimated, we have learned a thing or two since then. And it is not a little thing to have discovered that, though their hearts were right and their intentions good, our forefathers were not so abnormally virtuous and wise as to entitle them or us to an exclusive and proscriptive patent of superiority. We glory in them, but while we revere them as the fosterers and perpetuators of that fine, energetic, high-minded, probing spirit which we call the touch-stone of Americanism, we are prepared, with some reluctance, yet frankly, when cornered, to admit that they did not possess a monopoly of righteousness or knowledge.

I shall assume, then, that you, in common with other citizens, have reached this rationally patriotic point of view and are willing to agree that we are not, as a nation, above criticism. If you are still inclined to regard us, the plain people of these United States, as a mighty phalanx of Sir Galahads in search of the Holy Grail, the citation of a few facts may act aperiently on your mind and wash away the cobwebs of hallucination. For instance, to begin from the political standpoint, our acquirement of Texas and other territory once belonging to Mexico suggests the predatory methods of the Middle Ages rather than an aspiring and sensitive national public temper. The government of our large cities has from time to time been so notoriously corrupt as to indicate at least an easy-going, shiftless, civic spirit in the average free-born municipal voter. It is a matter of common knowledge that in the legislative bodies of all our States there is a certain number of members whose action in support of or against measures is controlled by money bribes. From the point of view of morals, statistics show that poverty and crime, drunkenness and licentiousness in our large cities are little less rife than in the great capitals of Europe; and you have merely to read the newspapers to satisfy yourself that individuals from the population of the small towns and of the country districts from the eastern limit of Maine to the southwestern coast of California are capable of monstrous murders, rank thefts, and a sensational variety of ordinary human vices. It were easy to illustrate further, but this should convince you that the patriotic enthusiast who would prove the people of the United States to be a cohort of angels of light has verily a task compared with which the labors of Sisyphus and other victims of impossibility fade into ease. Even our public schools, that favorite emblem of our omniscience, have been declared by au-

thority to merit interest but by no means gro-
velling admiration on the part of the effete peoples of Europe.

We will proceed then on the understanding
that, whatever its past, the present civilization
of the United States reveals the every-day human being in his or her infinite variety, and that
the true American must grasp this fact in order
to fulfil his destiny. If our nation is to be a lamp
to the civilized world, it will be because we prove
with time that poor human nature, by virtue of
the leaven called Americanism, has reached a
higher plane of intelligent virtue and happiness
than the world has hitherto attained. Who then
is the true American? And what are the signs
which give us hope that the people of the
United States are capable of accomplishing this
result? What, too, are the signs which induce
our censors and critics to shake their heads and
refuse to acknowledge the probability of it?

To *A Young Man* wishing to be an American. II.

I WILL begin with the inverse process and indicate a list of those who are not true Americans, and yet who are so familiar types in our national community that the burden of proof is on the patriot to show that they are not essentially representative.

No. 1. *The Plutocratic Gentleman of Leisure who Amuses Himself.*—Here we have a deliberate imitation of a well-known figure of the older civilizations. The grandfather by superior ability, industry, and enterprise has accumulated a vast fortune. His grandchildren, nurtured with care, spend their golden youth in mere extravagant amusement and often in dissipation. There are many individuals in our so-called leisure class who devote their lives to intelligent and useful occupation, but there is every reason for asserting that the point of view of the child of fortune in this country is significantly that of the idler —and a more deplorable idler than he of the aristocracies of Europe on whom he models himself for the reason that the foreigner is less indifferent than he to intellectual interests. Is there any body of people in the world more contemptible, and any body among us more useless as an inspiring product of Americanism, than the pleasure-seeking, unpatriotic element of the very rich who, under the caption of our best society, arrogate social distinction by reason of their vulgar ostentation of wealth, their extravagant methods of entertainment and their aimless pleasure-loving lives? To vie with each other in lavish outlay, to visit Europe with frequency, to possess steam-yachts, to bribe custom-house officers, to sneer at our institutions and, save by an occasional check, to ignore all the duties of citizenship, is an off-handed epitome of their existence. And in it all they are merely copy-cats —servile followers of the aristocratic creed, but without the genuine prestige of the old-time nobilities. And in the same breath let me not forget the women.

[*Note.*—"I was afraid you were going to," said my wife, Josephine. "Women count for so much here, and yet their heads seem to become hopelessly turned as soon as they are multi-millionaires."]

Women indeed count for much here, and yet

it is they even more than the men who are responsible for and encourage the mere pleasure-
loving life among the leisure class. A ceaseless
round of every variety of money-consuming,
vapid amusement occupies their days and nights
from January to January, and for what purpose?
To marry their daughters to foreign noblemen?
To breed scandal by pursuing intimacies with
other men than their husbands? To demonstrate
that the American woman, when she has all the
opportunities which health, wealth, and leisure
can bestow, is content to become a mere quick-
witted, shallow voluptuary?

You will be told that these people are very
inconsiderable in number, that they really exercise a small influence, and that one is not to
judge the men and women of the United States
by them. It is true that they are not very nu-
merous, though their number seems to be increasing, and I am fain to believe that they are
not merely out of sympathy with, but alien in
character to, the American people as a whole;
and yet I cannot see why an unfriendly critic
should not claim that they are representative,
for they are the lineal descendants of the men
from every part of the land who have been the

most successful in the accumulation of wealth.
Their grandfathers were the pioneers whose
brains and sinews were stronger than their fellows in the struggle of nation-building; their
fathers were the keenest and not presumptively
the most dishonest men of affairs in the country. Though the plain people of the nation affect
to reprobate this class as un-American and evil,
yet the newspapers, who aim to be the exponents
of the opinions of the general mass and to cater
to their preferences, are constantly setting forth
the doings of the so-called multi-millionaires and
their associates with a journalistic gusto and re-
dundancy which reveals an absorbing interest and
satisfaction in their concerns on the part of the
everyday public.

Undeniably there are no laws which prohibit
the wealthy from squandering their riches in futile extravagance and wasting their time in empty
frivolities, nor is our leisure class peculiar in this
when compared with the corresponding class in
other countries, unless it be in a more manifest
bent toward civic imbecility. But, from the point
of view of human progress, is it not rather discouraging that the most financially prosperous
should aspire merely to mimic and outdo the

follies of courts, the heartless levity and extravagance of which have been among the instigators of popular revolution? Surely, if this is the best Americanism, if this is what democracy proffers as the flower of its crown of success, it were more satisfactory to the sensitive citizen to owe allegiance to some country where the pretensions to omniscient soul superiority were more commensurate with the results produced.

No. 2. *The Easy-going Hypocrite.*—Here is another slip from the tree of human nature, which flourishes on this soil with a sturdy growth. A large section of the American people has been talking for buncombe, not merely since years ago the member of Congress from North Carolina naïvely admitted that his remarks were uttered solely for the edification of the county of that name, and so supplied a descriptive phrase for the habit, but from the outset of our national responsibilities. To talk for effect with the thinly concealed purpose of deceiving a part of the American people all of the time has been and continues to be a favorite practice with many of the politicians of the country. Yet this public trick of proclaiming sentiments and opinions with the tongue in the cheek is the conspicuous

surface-symptom of a larger vice which is fitly
described as hypocrisy. There is a way of looking at this accusation which deprives it of part
of its sting, yet leaves us in a predicament not
very complimentary to our boasted sense of humor. It is that the free-born American citizen
means so well that he is habitually dazzled by
his own predilections toward righteousness into
utterances which he as a frail mortal cannot hope
to live up to, and consequently that he is prone
to express himself in terms which none but the
unsophisticated are expected to believe. In other
words, that he is an unconscious hypocrite.
However harmless this idiosyncrasy may have
been as a preliminary trick of expression, there
is no room for doubt that the plea of uncon-
sciousness must cease to satisfy the most indul-
gent moral philosopher after a very short time.
Yet we have persevered in the practice astonishingly, until it may be said that hyperbole is
the favorite form of public utterance on almost
any subject among a large class of individuals,
in the expectation that only a certain percentage
will not understand that the speaker or writer
is not strictly in earnest. In this manner the virtuous and the patriotic are enabled to give free

vent to their emotions and to set their fellow-
citizens and themselves highest among the people of the earth without other expenditure than
words, resolutions, or empty laws. The process
gently titillates the self-esteem of the performer
so that he almost persuades himself for the time
being that he believes what he is saying: He
appreciates that his hearers like better to have
their hopes rehearsed as realities at the expense
of veracity than to be reminded of imperfections
at the expense of pride: And he rejoices in those
whom he has fooled into believing that their
hopes have been realized, and that all the virtue
which he tremendously stands for is part and
parcel of the national equipment. Under the in-
sidious influence of this mode of enlightenment
the everyday keen American citizen goes about
with his head in the air, knowing in his secret
heart that one-half of what he hears from the
lips of those who represent him in public is buncombe, but content with the shadow for the substance, and wearing a chip on his shoulder as a
warning to those who would assert that we are
not really as virtuous and as noble as our spokes-
men have declared.

For instance, to return to the concrete, con-

sider the plight of a police commissioner in most
of our large cities. Those interested in the sup-
pression of vice appear before the legislature and
urge the maintenance of a vigorous policy. Acts
are passed by the law-makers manifesting the
intention of the community to wage vigorous
war against the social evil and the sale of liquor,
and prescribing unequivocal regulations. The
appointing power is urged to select a strong man
to enforce these laws. Supposing he does, what
follows? Murmurs and contemptuous abuse.
Murmurs from what is known as the hard-
headed, common-sense portion of the community, who complain that the strong man entrusted
with authority does not show tact; that what was
expected of him was judicious surface enforcement of the law sufficient to beguile reformers
and cranks, and give a semblance of improvement, not strict, literal compliance. They will
tell you that the social evil can no more be suppressed than water can be prevented from running down hill, and that the explicit language
of the statutes was framed for the benefit of
clergymen, and that no one else with common
sense supposed it would be enforced to the letter
by any intelligent official. The very legislators

who voted to pass the laws will shrug their shoulders rancorously and confide to you the same thing; yet in another breath assert to their constituents that they have fought the fight in defence of white-robed chastity and the sacred sanctity of the home.

Now, is this Americanism, the very best Americanism? Surely not. It has an Anglo-Saxon flavor about it which it is easy to recognize as foreign and imported. Englishmen have been asserting for centuries that they were fighting the fight in defence of white-robed chastity and the sanctity of the home, to the amusement of the rest of the world, for in spite of the fact that the laws demand a vigorous policy and the British matron and the Sunday-school Unions declare that the home is safe, those familiar with facts know that London is one of the most disgustingly impure cities in the world, and that the youth let loose upon its streets is in very much the same predicament as Daniel in the den of lions, without the same certainty of rescue. And why? Because the hard-headed, common-sense British public sanctions hypocrisy. They tell you that they are doing their utmost to crush the evil. This is for the marines, the

British matron, and the Sunday-school Unions.
But let a strong man attempt to banish from
the streets the shoals of women of loose character, and what an unmistakable murmur would
arise. How long would he remain in office?

It may be that the social evil can no more be
suppressed than water can be prevented from
running down hill. That is neither here nor
there for the purposes of this illustration. But
to demand the passage of laws, and then to
abuse and undermine the influence of those who
try to enforce them is a vice more subversive
to national character than the fault of Mary
Magdalene and her unpenitent successors, both
male and female.

Take, again, our custom-house regulations
concerning persons returning home from abroad.
The law demands a certain tariff, yet it is notorious that a large number of so-called respectable people are able to procure free entry for
their effects by bribes to the subordinates. And
why? Because those who passed the law devised
it to cajole a certain portion of the community;
but those charged with the enforcement of it, in
deference to its unpopularity, are expected to
make matters at the port smooth for travellers

with easy-going consciences. Hence the continued existence at the New York Custom-house
of the shameless bribe-taker in all his disgusting
variety. Authority from time to time puts on a
semblance of integrity and discipline, but the
home-comer continues to gloat over the old
story of double deceit, his own and another's.
Is this the best Americanism? Yet these are
American citizens who offer the bribe, who
pocket it, and who allow the abuse to exist by
solemnly or good-naturedly ignoring it. Consider the diversity of our divorce laws. It is indeed true that opinions differ as to what are and
what are not suitable grounds for divorce, so
that uniformity of legislation in the different
States is difficult of attainment; yet there is reason to believe that progress toward this would
be swifter were it not for the convenience of the
present system which allows men and women
who profess orthodoxy a loop-hole of escape to
a less rigorous jurisdiction when the occasion
arises. Similarly, in the case of corporation laws,
it is noticeable that not far removed from those
communities where paid-up capital stock and
other assurances of good faith are required from
incorporators, some State is to be found where

none of these restrictions exist. Thus an appearance of virtue is preserved, self-consciousness of virtue flattered, a certain number deluded, and yet all the conveniences and privileges of a hard-headed, easy-going civilization are kept within reaching distance.

No. 3. *The Worshipper of False Gods.*—It is a commonplace of foreign criticism that the free-born American is insatiate for money, and that everything else pales into insignificance before the diameter of the mighty dollar. That is the favorite taunt of those who do not admire our institutions and behavior, and the favorite note of warning of those who would fain think well of us. No one can deny that the influence and power of money in this country during the last thirty years have been enormous. One reason for this is obvious. The magnificent resources of a huge territory have been developed during that period. Men have grown rich in a night, and huge fortunes have been accumulated with a rapidity adapted not merely to dazzle and stir to envy other nations, but to turn the heads of our own people. We have become one of the wealthiest civilizations, and our multi-millionaires are among the money magnates of the world. Yet popular sentiment in public utterance affects to despise money, and inclines to abuse those who possess it. I write "affects," for here again the point of hypocrisy recurs to mind, and even you very likely would be prompt to remind me that, according to our vernacular, to make one's pile and make it quickly is a widespread touch-stone of ambition. True enough it is that there has been, and is, room for reproach in the aggressiveness of this tendency, and yet the seeming hypocrisy is once more unconscious in that the popular point of view intends to be sincere, but the situation has been too dazzling for sober brains and high resolves. For let it be said that keenness of vision and a capacity for escaping from the trammels of conventional and inveterate delusions are essentially American traits, and as a consequence no one more clearly than the American citizen appreciates the importance of material resources as a factor of happy living, and none so definitely as he refuses to be discouraged by the priestly creed that only a few can be comfortable and happy in this life and that the poor and miserable will be recompensed hereafter for their earthly travails. His doctrine is that he desires, if possible, to be one of that comfortable and happy few, and in the exuberance of his consciousness that human life is absorbing, he fortifies the capacity to make the most of it by the quaint, convincing statement that we shall be a long time dead. His quick-witted, intelligent repugnance to the old theory that the mass should be cajoled into dispensing with earthly comforts has helped to give a humorous, material twist to his words; and yet, I venture to assert, has left his finer instincts unperverted, except in the case of the individual. This combination of an extraordinary opportunity and a shrewd intelligence has, however, it must be admitted, produced a considerable and sorry crop of individuals guided by the principle that wealth is the highest good, and should be sought at the expense of every scruple. Their many successes in the accomplishment of this single purpose have served to create the impression that the whole nation is thus diseased, and have done the greater harm of dwarfing many an aspiring nature, spell-bound by the cloud-capped towers and gorgeous palaces which sheer money-making has established. As a result the best Americanism is menaced both by the example of accumulation without conscience, and

the dangerous public atmosphere which this gen-
erates, in that the common eye is caught by the
brilliance of the spectacle, and the common mind
lured to meditate imitation at every sacrifice. So
they say of us that the American hero is the man
of material successes, "the smart man" who "gets
there" by hook or crook, and that we are content
to ask no embarrassing questions as to ways and
means, provided the pecuniary evidences of attainment are indisputable. The patriotic American resents this as a libel, and maintains that this
type of hero-worship is but a surface indication of
the public soul, just as the horrors of the divorce
court are but a surface indication of the general
conditions of married life. Yet the patriot must
admit that there is danger to the noble aspirations which we claim to cherish as Americans
from the bright, keen, easy-going, metallic, practical, hard-headed, humorous citizen, male and
female, whose aim is simply to push ahead, at
any cost, and who in the process does not hesitate to part with his spiritual properties as being
cumbersome, unremunerative and somewhat ridiculous. The materialist is no new figure in human civilization. "Eat, drink, and be merry, for
to-morrow we die," is but the ancient synonyme

for "we shall be a long time dead." A deep, abiding faith in the serious purposes of humanity has ever been obvious to us Americans as a national possession, however foreigners may deny it to us, but the American nature is at the same time, as I have suggested, essentially practical, level-headed, and inquiring, and is ever ready with a shrewd jest to dispute the sway of traditions founded on cant or out-worn ideas. It behooves you then, if you would be a true American, to beware overstepping the limit which separates aspiring, intelligent, winsome common-sense from the philosophy of mere materialism. There lies one of the great perils of democracy; and unless the development of democracy be toward higher spiritual experiences, Americanism must prove a failure. Keen enjoyment of living is a noble thing, so too is the ambition to overcome material circumstances, and to command the fruits of the earth. A realization of the possibility of this, and an emancipation from dogmas which foreordained him to despair, has evolved the alert, independent, progressive American citizen, and side by side with him the individual whom the less enlightened portion of the community have enshrined in their hearts under the caption of a smart man. This popular hero, with his taking guise of easy-going good nature, assuring his admirers by way of flippant disposition of the claims of conscience and aspiration that "it will be all the same a hundred years hence" is the kind of American whom every patriot should seek to discredit and avoid imitating.

HE foregoing suggestions will suffice, I think, to demonstrate to you that we are not uniformly a nation of Sir Galahads, and that certain types of Americanism, if encouraged and perpetuated, are likely to impair the value and force of our civilization. But having dispelled the hallucination that we are uniformly irreproachable, I would remind you that, in order to be a good American, it is even more necessary for you to appreciate the fine traits of your countrymen than to be keenly alive to their shortcomings. There are two ways of looking at any community, as there are two ways of looking at life. The same landscape may appear to the same gaze brilliant, inspiring, and interesting, or flat, homely, and unsuggestive, according as the eye of the onlooker be healthy or jaundiced. It is easy to fix one's attention on the vulgar and heartless ostentation of the rich, on the cheapness and venality of some of our legislators, on the evidences of hypocrisy and false hero-worship, materialism, and superficiality of a portion

of our population, and in doing so to forget and
overlook the efficacy and finer manifestations of
the people whose lives are the force and bul-
wark of the state. It is easy to go through the
streets of a large city and note only the noise
and smoke and stir, coarse circumstance and
coarser crime, neglecting to remember that be-
neath this kernel of hard, real life the human
heart is beating high and warm with the hopes
and desires of the spirit. It is not necessary for
a human being, it is essentially not necessary
for an American, to look at life from the point
of view of what the eye beholds in the hours of
soul-torpor. True is it that Americanism stands
to-day as almost synonymous with the struggle
of democracy, and that the equal development
of the life of the whole people for the common
good is what most deeply concerns us; but this
does not mean that it is right or American to
adhere to what is ordinary and low, because it
is still inevitable that the ideals and standards
of the mass should not be those of the finest
spirits. It was an American who bade you hitch
your wagon to a star, and you have only to re-
flect in order to recall the spiritual vigor, the
righteous force of will, the strength of aspiring

mind, the patriotic courage, the tireless soul-struggle of the early generations of choicely educated, simply nurtured Americans. Their thought and conscience, true and star-seeking even in its limitations, laid the foundations of law and order, of civic liberty and private welfare, of national honor and domestic repute. Their enterprise and perseverance, their grit and suppleness of intelligence wrested our broad Western acreage from the savage and—

[*Note.*—I was here interrupted in the fervor of this genuine peroration by my wife Josephine's exclamation, "Oh, how atrociously they abused and persecuted those poor Indians, shunting them off from reservation to reservation, cheating them out of their lands and furs!"

It is not agreeable to be held up in this high-wayman fashion when one is warming to a subject, but there is a melancholy truth in Josephine's statement which cannot be utterly contradicted. Still this is what I said to her: "My dear, I had hoped you understood that I had referred sufficiently to our national delinquencies, and that I was trying to depict to my correspondent the other side of the case. However just and appropriate your criticism might be under other circumstances, I can only regard it now as misplaced and unfortunate." I spoke with appropriate dignity. "Hoity, toity, toity me!" she responded. "I won't say another word."]

—wrested our broad Western acreage from the savage, and in less than half a century transformed it into a thriving, bustling, forceful civilization. Their ingenuity, their restless spirit of inquiry, their practical skill, their impatience of delay and love of swift decisive action have erected countless monuments in huge new cities founded in the twinkling of an eye, in the marvellous useful inventions which have revolutionized the methods of the world, the cotton-gin, the steamboat, the telegraph, the telephone, the palace-car—in the eager response made to the call of patriotism when danger threatened the existence of their country, and in the strong, original, clear-thinking, shrewdly acting, quaint personalities which have sprung from time to time from the very soil, as it were, in full mental panoply like the warriors of the Cadmean seed. Their stern sense of responsibility, their earnest desire for self-improvement, their ambitious zeal to acquire and to diffuse knowledge have founded, fostered, and supported the system of public schools and well-organized colleges which exist to-day in almost every portion of the country. The possessors of these qualities were Americans—the best Americans. Their plan of life was neither cheap nor shallow, but steadfast, aspiring, strong, and patient. From small beginnings, by industry and fortitude, they fought their way to success, and produced the powerful and vital nation whose career the world is watching with an interest born of the knowledge that it is humanity's latest and most important experiment. The development of the democratic principle is at the root of Americanism, but whoever, out of deference to what may be called practical considerations, abates one jot the fervor of his or her desire to escape from the commonplace, or who, in other words, forsakes his ideals and is content with a lower aim and a lower outlook, in order to suit the average temper, is false to his birthright and to the best Americanism.

It has been one of the grievances of those, whose material surroundings have been more favorable and who have possessed more ostensible social refinement than the mass of the population, that they were regarded askance and excluded from public service and influence. There used to be some foundation for this charge, but the counter plea of lack of sympathy and distrust of country was still more true, and an explanation and, in a large measure, a justification of the prejudice. True strength and refinement of character has always in the end commanded the respect and admiration of our people, but they have been roughly suspicious of any class isolation or assumption of superiority. It has been difficult accordingly for that type of Americans who arrogated tacitly, but nevertheless plainly, the prerogatives of social importance, to take an active part in the responsibilities of citizenship. They have been mistrusted, and sneered at, and not always unjustly, for they have been prone to belittle our national institutions and to make sport of the social idiosyncrasies of their unconventional countrymen for the entertainment of foreigners. And yet the people have never failed to recognize and to reverence the fine emanations of the spirit as evidenced by our poets, historians, thinkers, or statesmen. Our forceful humanitarian and ethical movements, our most earnest reforms found their most zealous and untiring supporters among the rank and file of the people. Abraham Lincoln was understood last of all by the social aristocracy of the nation. Emerson's inspiration found an answering chord in every country town in New England. True it is that on the surface the popular judgment may often seem superficial and cheap in tone, but the wise American is chary of accepting surface ebullitions as the real index of the public judgment. He understands that mixed in with the unthinking and the degenerate is a rank and file majority of sober, self-respecting men and women, whose instincts are both earnest and original, and who are to be depended on in every serious emergency to think and act on the side of civilizing progress. It is the inability to appreciate this which breeds our civic censors, who are led by their lack of perspective to underestimate the character of the people and to foretell the ultimate failure of our experiment.

The increase of wealth and a wider familiarity with luxury and comfort through the country has made a considerable and more important class of those whose material and social surroundings are exceptional. The participation of the citizens of this class in the affairs of government is no longer discouraged—on the contrary, it is welcomed by the community. Indeed, many men have secured nomination and election to office solely because of their large means, which enabled them to control men and caucuses in their own favor.

[*Note.*—An appearance of spontaneity is preserved in these cases by the publication of a letter from leading citizens requesting the candidate to stand for office. He thereupon yields to the overwhelming invitation of the voters of the district, and his henchmen do the rest.]

But though the possession of wealth and social sophistication are no longer regarded as un-American, the public sentiment against open or tacit assumption of social superiority, or a lack of sympathy with democratic principles, is as strong as ever. It is incumbent, therefore, on you, if you would be an American in the best sense, to fix your ideal of life high, and at the same time to fix it in sympathy with the underlying American principle of a broad and progressive common humanity, free from caste or discriminating social conventions. It is not necessary for you to accept the standards and adopt the behavior of the superficial and imperfectly educated, but it is indispensable that you accept and act on the faith that your fellow-man is your brother, and that the attainment of a freer and more equal enjoyment of the privileges of life is essential to true human progress. We have, as I have intimated, passed through the pioneer stage of national development; we have tilled our fields, opened our mines, built our railroads, established our large cities—in short, have laid the foundations of a new and masterful civilization; it now remains for us to show whether we are capable of treating with originality the old problems which confront complex societies, and of solving them for the welfare of the public and the consequent elevation of individual character.

The originality and clearness of the American point of view has always been a salient national characteristic. Hitherto its favorite scope has been commercial and utilitarian. Yankee notions have been suggestive of sewing-machines, reapers, and labor-saving contrivances, or the mechanism of rushing trade. Now that

we have caught up with the rest of the world in
material progress and taught it many tricks, it
remains for the true American to demonstrate
equal sagacity and clear-headedness in dealing
with subtler conditions. To be sure the scope
of our originality has not been entirely directed
to things material, for we have ever asserted
with some vehemence our devotion to the things
of the spirit, squinting longingly at them even
when obliged to deplore only a passing acquaintance with them because of lack of time. The
splendid superficiality of the army of youth of
both sexes in the department of intellectual and
artistic exertion, which has been one of the
notable features of the last thirty years, has
shown clearly enough the true temper and fibre
of our people. To regard this superficiality as
more than a transient symptom, and thereby to
lose sight of the genuine intensity of nature
which has animated it, would indicate the shallow observer. Our youth has been audacious,
self-confident, and lacking in thoroughness because of its zeal to assert and distinguish itself,
and thus has justly, in one sense, incurred the
accusation of being superficial, but it has incurred this partially because of its disposition

to maintain the privileges of individual judgments.

Our young men and women have been blamed for their lack of reverence and their readiness to form conclusions without adequate knowledge or study in the teeth of venerable opinion and convention. Indisputably they have erred in this respect, but indisputably also the fault is now recognized, and is being cured in the curriculum of education. Yet, evil as the fault is, the traits which seem to have nourished it—unwillingness to accept tradition and a searching, honest clearness of vision—are virtues of the first water, and typical of the best national character. There are many persons of education and refinement in our society who accept as satisfactory and indisputable the old forms and symbols which illustrate the experience, and have become the final word of the older civilizations in ethics, politics, and art. They would be willing that we should become a mere complement to the most highly civilized nations of Europe, and they welcome every evidence that we are becoming so. As I have already suggested to you, the nations of the world are all nearer akin in thought and impulse than formerly, but if our civilization is to stand for anything, it must be by our divergence from the conclusions of the past when they fail to pass the test of honest scrutiny, not by tame imitation. Profoundly necessary as it is that we should accept with reverence the truths of experience, and much as our students and citizens may learn from the wisdom and performance of older peoples, it behooves the American to prize and cherish his birthright of independent judgment and freedom from servile adherence to convention. Almost everything that has been truly vital in our production has borne the stamp of this birthright.

The American citizen of the finest type is essentially a man or woman of simple character, and the effect of our institutions and mode of thought, when rightly appreciated, is to produce simplicity. The American is free from the glamour or prejudice which results from the conscious or unconscious influence of the lay figures of the old political, social, or religious world, from the glamour of royalty and vested caste, of an established or dominant church, of aristocratic, monkish, or military privilege. He is neither impelled nor allured to subject the liberty of conscience or opinion to the conventions appurtenant to these former forces of society. For him the law of the state, in the making of which he has a voice, and the authority of his own judgment are the only arbiters of his conduct. He accords neither to fineness of race nor force of intellect the right of aristocratic exclusiveness which they have too often hitherto claimed. To the cloistered nun he devotes no special reverence; he sees in the haughty and condescending fine gentleman an object for the exercise of his humor, not of servility; he is indifferent to the claim of all who by reason of self-congratulation or ancient custom arrogate to themselves special privileges on earth, or special privileges in heaven. This temper of mind, when unalloyed by shallow conceit, begets a quiet self-respect and simple honesty of judgment, eminently serviceable in the struggle to live wisely.

To the best citizens of every nation the most interesting and vital of all questions is what we are here for, what men and women are seeking to accomplish, what is to be the future of human development. For Americans of the best type, those who have learned to be reverent without losing their independence and without sacrifice of originality, the problem of living is simplified through the elimination of the influence of these symbols and conventions. Their outlook is not confused or deluded by the specious dogmas of caste. They perceive that the attainment of the welfare and happiness of the inhabitants of earth is the purpose of human struggle, and that the free choice and will of the majority as to what is best for humanity as a whole is to be the determining force of the future. To those who argue that the majority must always be wrong, and that as a corollary the will of the cheap man will prevail, this drift of society is depressing. The good American in the first place, recognizing the inevitability of this drift, declines to be depressed; and in the second, without subscribing to the doctrine that the majority must be wrong, exercises the privilege of his own independent judgment, subject only to the statute law and his conscience.

There is a noble strength of position in this; there is a danger, too, in that it suggests a lack of definiteness of standard. Yet this want of precision is preferable to the tyranny of hard and fast prescription. It is clear, for instance, that if the men and women of civilization are determined to modify their divorce laws so as to allow the annulment of marriage when either party is weary of the compact, no canon or anathema of the church will restrain them. Nor, on the other hand, will the mere whim or volition of an easy-going majority force them to do so. The judgment of men and women untrammelled by precedent and tradition and seeking simply to ascertain what is best and wisest for all will settle the question. Though the majority will be the force that puts any law into effect, the impulse must inevitably come from the higher wisdom of the few, and that higher wisdom in America works in the interest of a broad humanity, free from the delusions of outworn culture. The wisdom of the few may not seem to guide, but in the end the mass listens to true counsel. Honesty toward self and toward one's fellow-man, without fear or favor, is the leavening force of the finest Americanism, and, if persevered in, will lead the many, sooner or later, with a compelling power far beyond that of thrones and hierarchies. The wise application of this doctrine of the search for the common good in the highest terms of earthly condition to the whole range of economic, social, and political questions is what demands to-day the interest and attention of earnest Americans. The problems relating to capital and labor, to the restraint of the money power, to the government of our cities, to the education of all classes, to the status of divorce, to the treatment of paupers and criminals, to the wise control of the sale of liquor, to equitable taxation, and to a variety of kindred matters are ripe for the scrutiny of independent, sagacious thought and action. To the consideration of these subjects the best national intelligence is beginning to turn with a fresh vigor and efficiency, but none too soon. Though democracy and Americanism have become largely identical, the spread of the creed of a broader humanity in the countries of civilization where autocratic forms of government still obtain, has been so signal and productive of results that the American may well ask himself or herself if our people have not been slovenly and vain-glorious along the paths where it seemed to be their prerogative to lead. Certainly in the matter of many of the civic and humanitarian problems which I have cited, we may fitly borrow from the recent and modern methods of those to whom we are apt to refer, in terms of condescending pity, as the effete dynasties of Europe. They have in some instances been more prompt than we to recognize the trend of our and the world's new faith.

To *A Young Man* wishing to be an American. IV.

IN this same connection I suggest to you that in the domain of literary art an Englishman—a colonist, it is true, and so a little nearer allied to us in democratic sentiment—has more clearly and forcibly than any one else expressed the spirit of the best Americanism—of the best world-temper of to-day. I refer to Rudyard Kipling. Human society has been fascinated by the virility and uncompromising force of his writings, but it has found an equal fascination in the deep, simple, sham-detesting sympathy with common humanity which permeates them. He has been the first to adopt and exalt the idea of the brotherhood of man without either condescension or depressing materialistic realism. He has interpreted the poetry of "the trivial round and common task" without suggesting impending soup, blankets, and coals on earth and reward in heaven on the one hand, or without emphasizing the dirtiness of the workman's blouse on the other. His imagery, his symbols and his point of view are essentially alien to

those of social convention and caste. Yet his heroes of the engine-room, the telegraph-station,
the Newfoundland Banks, and the dreary ends
of the earth, democratic though they are to the
core, appeal to the imagination by their stimulating human qualities no less than the bearers
of titles and the aristocratic monopolists of culture and aspiration who have been the leading
figures in the poetry and fiction of the past.
Strength, courage, truth, simplicity and loving-
kindness are still their salient qualities—the
qualities of noble manhood; he expounds them
to us by the force of his sympathy, which clothes
them with no impossible virtues, yet shows
them, in the white light of performance, men no
less entitled to our admiration than the Knights
of King Arthur or any of the other superhuman
figures of traditional æsthetic culture. He recognizes the artistic value of the workaday life in
law courts and hospitals and libraries and mines
and factories and camps and lighthouses and
ocean steamers and railroad trains, as a stimulus
to and rectifier of poetic imagination, negativing
the theory that men and women are to seek inspiration solely from what is dainty, exclusive,
elegantly romantic, or rhapsodically star-gazing

in human conditions and thought. This is of the
essence of the American idea, which has been,
however, slow to subdue imagination, which is
the very electric current of art, to its use by reason chiefly of the seeming discord between it
and common life, and partly from the reluctance
of the world to renounce its diet of highly col-
ored court, heaven and fairy-land imagery; partly, too, because so many of the best poets and
writers of America have adopted traditional symbols. The great New England writers, who have
just passed away, were, however, the exponents
of the simple life, of high religious and intellectual thought amid common circumstance. They
stood for noble ideals as the privilege of all. Yet
their mental attitude, though scornful of pomp
and materialism, was almost aristocratic; at least
it was exclusive in that it was not wholly human, savoring rather of the ascetic star-gazer than
the full-blooded appreciator of the boon of life.
Their passion was pure as snow, but it was thin.
Yet the central tenet of their philosophy, independent naturalness of soul, is the necessary complement to the broad human sympathy which
is of the essence of modern art. The difficulty
which imagination finds in expressing itself in

the new terms is natural enough, for the poet and painter and musician are seemingly deprived of color, the color which we associate with mystic elegance and aristocratic prestige. Yet only seemingly. Externals may have lost the dignity and lustre of prerogative; but the essentials for color remain—the human soul in all its fervor —the striving world in all its joy and suffering. There is no fear that the tide of existence will be less intense or that the mind of man will degenerate in æsthetic appreciation, but it must be on new lines which only a master imbued with the value and the pathos of the highest life in the common life as a source for heroism can fitly indicate. There lies the future field for the poet, the novelist, and the painter—the idealization of the real world as it is in its highest terms of love and passion, struggle, joy, and sorrow, free from the condescension of superior castes and the mystification of the star-reaching introspective culture which seeks only personal exaltation, and excludes sympathy with the everyday beings and things of earth from its socalled spiritual outlook.

To *A Political Optimist.*
I.

I APPROVE of you, for I am an optimist myself in regard to human affairs, and can conscientiously agree with many of the patriotic statements concerning the greatness of the American people contained in your letter. Your letter interested me because it differed so signally in its point of view from the others which I received at the same time—the time when I ran for Congress as a Democrat in a hopelessly Republican district and was defeated. The other letters were gloomy in tone. They deplored the degeneracy of our political institutions, and argued from the circumstance that the voters of my district preferred "a hack politician" and "blatant demagogue" to "an educated philosopher" (the epithets are not mine) that we were going to the dogs as a nation. The prophecy was flattering to me in my individual capacity, but it has not served to soil the limpid, sunny flow of my philosophy. I was gratified, but not convinced. I behold the flag of my country still with moistened eyes—the eyes of pride, and I continue to bow affably to my successful rival.

Your suggestion was much nearer the truth. You indicated with pardonable levity that I was not elected because the other man received more votes. I smiled at that as an apt statement. You went on to take me to task for having given the impression in my published account of the political canvass not merely that I ought to have been elected, but that the failure to elect me was the sign of a lack of moral and intellectual fibre in the American people. If I mistake not, you referred to me farther on in the style of airy persiflage as a "holier than thou," a journalistic, scriptural phrase in current use among so-called patriotic Americans. And then you began to argue: You requested me to give us time, and called attention to the fact that the English system of rotten boroughs in vogue fifty years ago was worse than anything we have to-day. "We are a young and impetuous people," you wrote, "but there is noble blood in our veins—the blood which inspired the greatness of Washington and Hamilton and Franklin and Jefferson and Webster and Abraham Lincoln. Water does not run up hill. Neither do the

American people move backward. Their destiny is to progress and to grow mightier and mightier. And those who seek to retard our national march by cynical insinuations and sneers, by scholastic sophistries and philosophical wimwams, will find themselves inevitably under the wheels of Juggernaut, the car of republican institutions."

Philosophical wimwams! You sought to wound me in a tender spot. I forgive you for that, and I like your fervor. Those rotten boroughs have done yeoman service. They are on the tongue of every American citizen seeking for excuses for our national short-comings. But for my dread of a mixed metaphor I would add that they are moth-eaten and threadbare.

Your letter becomes then a miscellaneous catalogue of our national prowess. You instance the cotton-gin, the telegraph, the sewing-machine, and the telephone, and ask me to bear witness that they are the inventions of free-born Americans. You refer to the heroism and vigor of the nation during the Civil War, and its mighty growth in prosperity and population since; to the colleges and academies of learning, to the hospitals and other monuments of intelligent philanthropy, to the huge railroad systems, public works, and private plants which have come into being with mushroom-like growth over the country. You recall the energy, independence, and conscientious desire for Christian progress among our citizens, young and old, and, as a new proof of their disinterested readiness to sacrifice comfort for the sake of principle, you cite the recent emancipation of Cuba. Your letter closes with a Fourth of July panegyric on the heroes on land and sea of the war with Spain, followed by an exclamation point which seems to say, "Mr. Philosopher, put that in your pipe and smoke it."

I have done so, and admit that there is a great deal to be proud of in the Olla Podrida of exploits and virtues which you have set before me. Far be it from me to question the greatness and capacity of your and my countrymen. But while my heart throbs agreeably from the thrill of sincere patriotism, I venture to remind you that cotton-gins, academies of learning, and first-class battle-ships have little to do with the matter in question. Your mode of procedure reminds me of the plea I have heard used to obtain partners for a homely girl—that she is good to her mother. I notice that you include our political sanctity by a few sonorous phrases in the dazzling compendium of national success, but I also notice that you do not condescend to details. That is what I intend to do, philosophically yet firmly.

To begin with, I am not willing to admit that I was piqued by my failure to be elected to Congress. I did not expect to succeed, and my tone was, it seems to me, blandly resigned and even rather grateful than otherwise that such a serious honor had not been thrust upon me. Success would have postponed indefinitely the trip to Japan on which my wife, Josephine, had set her heart. In short, I supposed that I had concealed alike grief and jubilation, and taken the result in a purely philosophic spirit. It seems though that you were able to read between the lines—that is what you state—and to discern my condescending tone and lack of faith in the desire and intention of the plain people of these United States to select competent political representatives. I can assure you that I have arrived at no such dire state of mind, and I should be sorry to come to that conclusion; but, though a philosopher, and hence, politically speaking, a worm, I have a proper spirit of my own and beg to inform you that the desire and intention of our fellow-countrymen, whether plain or otherwise, so to do is, judging by their behavior, open to grave question. So you see I stand at bay almost where you supposed, and there is a definite issue between us. Judging by their behavior, remember. Judging by their words, butter would not melt in their mouths. I merely wish to call your attention to a few notorious facts in defence of my attitude of suspicion.

[*Note.*—"Josephine," said I to my wife at this point, "please enumerate the prominent elective offices in the gift of the American people."

My wife rose and after a courtesy, which was mock deferential, proceeded to recite with the glib fluency of a school-girl the following list—"Please, sir,

> President.
> Senators of the United States (elected by the State legislatures).
> Representatives of the United States.
> State Senators.
> State Assemblymen or Representatives.
> Aldermen.

Members of the City Council.

Members of the School Committee."

"Correct, Josephine. I pride myself that, thanks to my prodding, you are beginning to acquire some rudimentary knowledge concerning the institutions of your country. Thanks to me and Professor Bryce. Before Professor Bryce wrote 'The American Commonwealth,' American women seemed to care little to know anything about our political system. They studied more or less about the systems of other countries, but displayed a profound ignorance concerning our own form of government. But after an Englishman had published a book on the subject, and made manifest to them that our institutions were reasonably worthy of attention, considerable improvement has been noticeable. But I will say that few women are as well posted as you, Josephine."

She made another mock deferential courtesy. "Thank you, my lord and master; and lest you have not made it sufficiently clear that my superiority in this respect is due to your—your nagging, I mention again that you are chiefly responsible for it. It bores me, but I submit to it."

"Continue then your docility so far as to write the names which you have just recited on separate slips of paper and put them in a proper receptacle. Then I will draw one as a preliminary step in the political drama which I intend to present for the edification of our correspondent."

Josephine did as she was bid, and in the process, by way of showing that she was not such a martyr as she would have the world believe, remarked, "If you had really been elected, Fred, I think I might have made a valuable political ally. What I find tedious about politics is that they 're not practical—that is for me. If you were in Congress now, I should make a point of having everything political at the tip of my tongue."

"Curiously enough, my dear, I am just going to give an object lesson in practical politics, and you as well as our young friend may be able to learn wisdom from it. Now for a blind choice!" I added, putting my hand into the work-bag which she held out.

"Aldermen!" I announced after scrutinizing the slip which I had drawn. Josephine's nose went up a trifle.

"A very fortunate and comprehensive selection," I asserted. "The Alderman and the influences which operate upon and around him lie at the root of American practical politics. And from a careful study of the root you will be able to decide how genuinely healthy and free from taint must be the tree—the tree which bears such ornamental flowers as Presidents and United States Senators, gorgeous blooms of apparent dignity and perfume."]

This being a drama, my young patriot, I wish to introduce you to the stage and the principal characters. The stage is any city in the United States of three hundred thousand or more inhabitants. It would be invidious for me to mention names where any one would answer to the requirements. Some may be worse than others, but all are bad enough. A bold and pessimistic beginning, is it not, my optimistic friend?

And now for the company. This drama differs from most dramatic productions in that it makes demands upon a large number of actors. To produce it properly on the theatrical stage would bankrupt any manager unless he were subsidized heavily from the revenues of the

twenty leading villains. The cast includes besides twenty leading villains, twelve low comedians, no hero, no heroine (except, incidentally,
Josephine); eight newspaper editors; ten thousand easy-going second-class villains; ten thousand patriotic, conscientious, and enlightened
citizens, including a sprinkling of ardent reformers; twenty-five thousand zealous, hide-
bound partisans; fifty thousand respectable,
well-intentioned, tolerably ignorant citizens who
vote but are too busy with their own affairs
to pay attention to politics, and as a consequence
generally vote the party ticket, or vote to please
a "friend"; ten thousand superior, self-centred
souls who neglect to vote and despise politics
anyway, among them poets, artists, scientists,
some men of leisure, and travellers; ten thousand enemies of social order such as gamblers,
thieves, keepers of dives, drunkards, and toughs;
and your philosopher.

A very large stock company. I will leave the
precise arithmetic to you. I wish merely to indicate the variegated composition of the average
political constituency, and to let you perceive
that the piece which is being performed is no
parlor comedy. It is written in dead earnest, and

it seems to me that the twenty leading villains, though smooth and in some instances aristocratic appearing individuals, are among the most dangerous characters in the history of this or any other stage. But before I refer to them more particularly I will make you acquainted with our twelve low comedians—the Board of Aldermen.

It is probably a surprise to you and to Josephine that the Aldermen are not the villains. Everything is comparative in this world, and, though I might have made them villains without injustice to such virtues as they possess, I should have been at a loss how to stigmatize the real promoters of the villainy. And after all there is an element of grotesque comedy about the character of Aldermen in a large American city. The indecency of the situation is so unblushing, and the public is so helpless, that the performers remind one in their good-natured antics of the thieves in Fra Diavolo; they get bolder and bolder and now barely take the trouble to wear the mask of respectability.

Have I written "thieves?" Patriotic Americans look askance at such full-blooded expressions. They prefer ambiguity, and a less harsh phraseology—"slight irregularities," "business misfortunes," "commercial usages," "professional services," "campaign expenses," "lack of fine sensibilities," "unauthenticated rumors." There are fifty ways of letting one's fellow-citizens down easily in the public prints and in private conversation. This is a charitable age, and the word thief has become unfamiliar except as applied to rogues who enter houses as a trade. The community and the newspapers are chary of applying it to folk who steal covertly but steadily and largely as an increment of municipal office. It is inconvenient to hurt the feelings of public servants, especially when one may have voted for them from carelessness or ignorance.

Here is a list of the twelve low comedians for your inspection:

Peter Lynch, no occupation.

James Griffin, stevedore.

William H. Bird, real estate.

John S. Maloney, saloon-keeper.

David H. Barker, carpenter.

Jeremiah Dolan, no occupation.

Patrick K. Higgins, junk dealer.

Joseph Heffernan, liquors.

William T. Moore, apothecary.

James O. Frost, paints and oils.

Michael O'Rourke, tailor.

John P. Driscoll, lawyer.

You will be surprised by my first statement regarding them, I dare say. Four of them, Peter Lynch, James Griffin, Jeremiah Dolan, and Michael O'Rourke neither drink nor smoke. Jeremiah Dolan chews, but the three others do not use tobacco in any form. They are patterns of Sunday-school virtue in these respects. This was a very surprising discovery to one of the minor characters in our drama—to two of them in fact—Mr. Arthur Langdon Waterhouse and his father, James Langdon Waterhouse, Esq. The young man, who had just returned from Europe with the idea of becoming United States Senator and who expressed a willingness to serve as a Reform Alderman while waiting, announced the discovery to his parent shortly before election with a mystified air.

"Do you know," said he to the old gentleman, who, by the way, though he has denounced every person and every measure in connection with our politics for forty years, was secretly pleased at his son's senatorial aspirations, "do

you know that some one told me to-day that
four of the very worst of those fellows have never
drunk a drop of liquor, nor smoked a pipe of
tobacco in their lives. Is n't it a curious circumstance? I supposed they were intoxicated most
of the time."

You will notice also that Peter Lynch and
Jeremiah Dolan have no occupation. Each of
them has been connected in some capacity with
the City Government for nearly twenty years,
and they are persons of great experience. They
have more than once near election time been amiably referred to in the press as "valuable public servants," and it must be admitted that they
are efficient in their way. Certainly, they know
the red tape of City Hall from A to Z, and understand how to block or forward any measure.
The salary of Alderman is not large—certainly
not large enough to satisfy indefinitely such
capable men as they, and yet they continue to
appear year after year at the same old stand.
Moreover, they resist vigorously every effort
to dislodge them, whether proceeding from political opponents or envious rivals of their own
party. A philosopher like myself, who is, politically speaking, a worm, is expected to believe

that valuable public servants retain office for the honor of the thing; but even a philosopher becomes suspicious of a patriot who has no occupation.

Next in importance are Hon. William H. Bird and Hon. John P. Driscoll. It is a well-known axiom of popular government that citizens are called from the plough or counting-room to public office by the urgent request of their friends and neighbors. As a fact, this takes place two or three times in a century. Most aspirants for office go through the form of having a letter from their friends and neighbors published in the newspapers, but only the very guileless portion of the public do not understand that the candidates in these cases suggest themselves. It is sometimes done delicately, as, for instance, in the case of young Arthur Langdon Waterhouse of whom I was writing just now. He let a close friend intimate to the ward committee that he would like to run for Alderman, and that in consideration thereof his father would be willing to subscribe two thousand dollars to the party campaign fund. It seems to a philosopher that a patriotic people should either re-edit its political axioms or live up to them.

Now Hon. William H. Bird and Hon. John P. Driscoll never go through the ceremony of being called from the plough—in their case the ward bar-room. They announce six months in advance that they wish something, and they state clearly what. They are perpetual candidates for, or incumbents of, office, and to be elected or defeated annually costs each of them from two to four thousand dollars according to circumstances. One of them has been in the Assembly, the Governor's Council, and in both branches of the City Government; the other a member of the Assembly, a State Senator, and an Alderman, and both of them are now glad to be Alderman once more after a desperate Kilkenny contest for the nomination. They are called Honorable by the reporters; and philosophers and other students of newspapers are constantly informed that Hon. William H. Bird has done this, and Hon. John P. Driscoll said that.

These four are the big men of the Board. The others are smaller fry; ambitious and imitative, but less experienced and smooth and audacious. Yet the four have their virtues, too. It is safe to state that no one of them would take anything beyond his reach. Moreover, if you, a patriot,

or I, a philosopher, were to find himself alone in
a room with one of them and had five thousand
dollars in bills in a pocket-book and the fact were
known to him, he would make no effort to possess himself of the money. We should be absolutely safe from assault or sleight of hand. Whoever would maintain the opposite does not appreciate the honesty of the American people. If,
on the other hand, under similar circumstances,
the right man were to place an envelope containing one thousand dollars in bills on the table
and saunter to the window to admire the view,
the packet would disappear before he returned
to his seat and neither party would be able to
remember that it ever was there. I do not intend
to intimate that this is the precise method of procedure; I am merely explaining that our comedians have not the harsh habits of old-fashioned
highwaymen.

Then again, there are people so fatuous as to
believe that Aldermen are accustomed to help
themselves out of the city treasury. That is a
foolish fiction, for no Alderman could. The City
Hall is too bulky to remove, and all appropria-
tions of the public money are made by draft and
have to be accounted for. If any member of the

Board were to make a descent on the funds in the safe, he would be arrested as a lunatic and sent to an insane asylum.

As for the other eight low comedians, it happens in this particular drama that I would be unwilling to make an affidavit as to the absolute integrity of any one of them. But there are apt to be two or even three completely honest members of these august bodies, and two or three more who are pretty honest. A pretty honest Alderman is like a pretty good egg. A pretty honest Alderman would be incapable of touching an envelope containing one thousand dollars, or charging one hundred in return for his support to a petition for a bay-window; but if he were in the paint and oil business or the lumber trade, or interested in hay and oats, it would be safe to assume that any department of the City Government which did not give his firm directly or indirectly a part of its trade would receive no aldermanic favors at his hands. Then again, a pretty honest Alderman would allow a friend to sell a spavined horse to the city.

To *A Political Optimist.*
II.

HAVING hinted gently at the leading characteristics of the twelve low co-medians, I am ready now to make you acquainted with the twenty leading villains. There is something grimly humorous in the spectacle of a dozen genial, able-bodied, non-alcoholic ruffians levying tribute on a community too self-absorbed or too easy-going or too indifferent to rid itself of them. I find, on the other hand, something somewhat pathetic in the spectacle of twenty otherwise reputable citizens and capitalists driven to villainy by the force of circumstances. To be a villain against one's will is an unnatural and pitiable situation.

That one may smile, and smile, and be a villain!

Here is the list:

Thomas Barnstable, President of the People's Heat and Power Company.

William B. Wilcox, General Manager of the North Circuit Traction Company.

David J. Prendergast, Treasurer of the Underground Steam Company.

Porter King, President of the South Valley Railroad Company.

James Plugh, Treasurer of the Star Brewing Concern.

Ex-State Treasurer George Delaney Johnson, Manager of the United Gas Company.

Willis O. Golightly, Treasurer of the Consolidated Electric Works.

Hon. Samuel Phipps, President of the Sparkling Reservoir Company.

P. Ashton Hall, President of the Rapid Despatch Company.

Ex-Congressman Henry B. Pullen, Manager of the Maguinnis Engine Works. And so on. I will not weary you with a complete category. It would contain the names of twelve other gentlemen no less prominent in connection with quasi-public and large private business corporations. With them should be associated one thousand easy-going, second-class villains, whose names are not requisite to my argument, but who from one year to another are obliged by the exigencies of business or enterprise to ask for licenses from the non-alcoholic, genial comedians, for permission to build a stable, to erect a bay-window, to peddle goods in the streets, to maintain a coal-hole, to drain into a sewer, to lay wires underground; in short, to do one or another of the many everyday things which can be done only by permission of the City Government. And the pity of it is that they all would rather not be villains.

[*Note.*—At the suggestion of Josephine I here enter a caveat for my and her protection. While I was enumerating the list of low comedians she interrupted me to ask if I did not fear lest one of them might sand-bag me some dark night on account of wounded sensibilities. She laughed, but I saw she was a little nervous.

"I have mentioned no real names," said I.

"That is true," she said, "but somehow I feel that the real ones might be suspicious that they were meant."

I told her that this was their lookout, and that, besides, they were much too secure in the successful performance of their comedy to go out of their way to assassinate a philosopher. "They would say, Josephine, that a philosopher cuts no ice, which is true, and is moreover a serious stigma to fasten on any patriotic man or woman." But now again she has brought me to book on the score of the feelings of the leading villains. She appreciates that we are on terms of considerable friendliness with some Presidents of corporations, and that though my list contains no real names, I may give offence. Perhaps she fears a sort of social boycott. Let me satisfy her scruples and do justice at the same time by admitting that not every President of a quasi-public corporation is a leading villain. Nor every Alderman a low comedian. That will let out all my friends. But, on the other hand, I ask the attention even of my friends to the predicament of Thomas Barnstable, President of the People's Heat and Power Company.]

Thomas Barnstable, the leading villain whose case I select for detailed presentation, has none of the coarser proclivities of David J. Prendergast, Treasurer of the Underground Steam Company. As regards David J. Prendergast, I could almost retract my allegation of pity and assert that he is a villain by premeditation and without compunction. That is, his method of dealing with the twelve low comedians is, I am told, conducted on a cold utilitarian basis without struggle of conscience or effort at self-justification. He says to the modern highwaymen, "Fix your price and let my bill pass. My time is valuable and so is yours, and the quicker we come to terms, the better for us both." What he says behind their backs is not fit for publication; but he recognizes the existence of the tax just as he recognizes the existence of the tariff, and he has no time to waste in considering the effect of either on the higher destinies of the nation.

Thomas Barnstable belongs to another school. He is a successful business man. In the ordinary meaning of the phrase, he is also a gentleman and a scholar. His word in private and in business life is as good as his bond; he respects the rights of the fatherless and the widow, and he is known favorably in philanthropic and religious circles. Having recognized the value of certain patents, he has become a large owner of the stock of the People's Heat and Power Company, and is the President of the corporation. Hitherto he has had plain sailing, municipally speaking. That is, the original franchise of the company was obtained from the city before he became President, and only this year for the first time has the necessity of asking for further privileges arisen. Moreover, he finds his corporation confronted by a rival, the Underground Steam Company.

Now here is a portion of the dialogue which took place five weeks before election between this highly respectable gentleman and his right-hand man, Mr. John Dowling, the efficient practical manager of the People's Company.

"Peter Lynch was here to-day," said Mr. Dowling.

"And who may Peter Lynch be?" was the dignified but unconcerned answer.

"Peter Lynch is Peter Lynch. Don't you know Peter? He's the Alderman from the fifth district. He has been Alderman for ten years, and so far as I can see, he is likely to continue to be Alderman for ten more."

"Ah."

"Peter was in good humor. He was smiling all over."

Mr. Dowling paused, so his superior said, "Oh!" Then realizing that the manager was still silent, as though expecting a question, he said, "Why did he come?"

"He wishes us to help him mend his fences. Some of them need repairing. The wear and tear of political life is severe."

"I see—I see," responded Mr. Barnstable, reflectively, putting his finger-tips together. "What sort of a man is Peter?"

Mr. Dowling hesitated a moment, merely because he was uncertain how to deal with such innocence. Having concluded that frankness was the most business-like course, he answered, bluffly, "He's an infernal thief. He's out for the stuff."

"The stuff? I see—I see. Very bad, very bad. It's an outrage that under our free form of government such men should get a foothold in our cities. I hope, Dowling, you gave him the cold shoulder, and let him understand that under no consideration whatever would we contribute one dollar to his support."

"On the contrary, I gave him a cigar and pumped him."

"Pumped him?"

"I wanted to find out what he knows."

"Dear me. And—er—what does he know?"

"He knows all about our bill, and he says he'd like to support it."

This was a shock, for the bill was supposed to be a secret.

"How did he find out about it?"

"Dreamt it in his sleep, I guess."

"I don't care for his support, I won't have it," said Mr. Barnstable, bringing his hand down forcibly on his desk to show his earnestness and indignation. "I wish very much, Mr. Dowling, that you had told him to leave the office and never show his impudent face here again."

There was a brief silence, during which Mr. Dowling fingered his watch-chain; then he said in a quiet tone, "He says that the Underground Steam Company is going to move heaven and earth to elect men who will vote to give them a location."

"I trust you let him know that the Underground Steam Company is a stock jobbing, disreputable concern with no financial status."

"It was n't necessary for me to tell him that. He knows it. He said he would prefer to side with us and keep them out of the streets, which meant of course that he knew we were able to pay the most if we chose. It seems Prendergast has been at him already."

"Disgusting! They both ought to be in jail."

"Amen. He says he gave Prendergast an evasive answer, and is to see him again next Tuesday. There's the situation, Mr. Barnstable. I tell you frankly that Lynch is an important man to keep friendly to our interests. He is very smart and well posted, and if we allow him to oppose us, we shall have no end of trouble. He is ready to take the ground that the streets ought not be dug up, and that a respectable corporation like ours should not be interfered with. Only he expects to be looked after in return. I deplore the condition of affairs as much as you do, but I tell you frankly that he is certain to go over to the other side and oppose us tooth and nail unless we show ourselves what he calls friendly to his 'interests.'"

"Then we'll prevent his election. I would subscribe money toward that myself."

The Manager coughed, by way perhaps of concealing a smile. "That would not be easy," he said. "And if it could be done, how should we be better off? Peter Lynch is only one of fifteen or twenty, many of whom are worse than he. By worse I mean equally unscrupulous and less efficient. Here, Mr. Barnstable, is a list of the candidates for Aldermen on both sides. I have been carefully over it and checked off the names of those most likely to be chosen, and I find that

it comprises twelve out-and-out thieves, five
sneak-thieves, as I call them, because they pilfer
only in a small way and pass as pretty honest;
four easy-going, broken-winded incapables, and
three perfectly honest men, one of them thoroughly stupid. Now, if we have to deal with
thieves, it is desirable to deal with those most
likely to be of real service. There are four men on
this list who can, if they choose, help us or hurt
us materially. If we get them, they will be able to
swing enough votes to control the situation; if
they 're against us, our bill will be side-tracked
or defeated, and the Underground Steam Company will get its franchise. That means, as you
know, serious injury to our stockholders. There 's
the case in a nut-shell."

"What are their names?" asked Mr. Barnstable, faintly.

"Peter Lynch, Jeremiah Dolan, William H.
Bird, and John P. Driscoll, popularly known in
the inner circles of City Hall politics as 'the big
four.' And they are—four of the biggest thieves
in the community."

"Dear me," said Mr. Barnstable. "And what
is it you advise doing?"

"Like the coon in the tree, I should say,

'Don't shoot and I 'll come down.' It 's best to have a clear understanding from the start."

"What I meant to ask was—er—what is it that this Peter Lynch wishes?"

"He uttered nothing but glittering generalities; that he desired to know who his friends were, and whether in case he were elected he could be of any service to our corporation. The English of that is, he expects in the first place a liberal subscription for campaign expenses— and after that retaining fees from time to time as our attorney or agent, which will vary in size according to the value of the services rendered."

A faint gleam of cunning hope appeared in Mr. Barnstable's eyes.

"Then anything we—er—contributed could properly be charged to attorney's fees?" he said by way of thinking aloud.

"Certainly—attorney's fees, services as agent, profit and loss, extraordinary expenses, machinery account, bad debts—there are a dozen ways of explaining the outlay. And no outlay may be necessary. A tip on the stock will do just as well."

"Dear, dear," reiterated Mr. Barnstable. "It 's a deplorable situation; deplorable and very awkward."

"And the awkward part is, that we're a dead cock in the pit if we incline to virtue's side."

Mr. Barnstable sighed deeply and drummed on his desk. Then he began to walk up and down. After a few moments he stopped short and said:

"I shall have to lay it before my directors, Dowling."

"Certainly, sir. But in general terms, I hope. A single—er—impractical man might block the situation until it was too late. Then the expense of remedying the blunder might be much greater."

Mr. Barnstable inclined his head gravely. "I shall consult some of the wisest heads on the Board, and if in their opinion it is advisable to conciliate these blackmailers, a formal expression of approval will scarcely be necessary."

A few days later the President sent for the Manager and waved him to a chair. His expression was grave—almost sad, yet resolute. His manner was dignified and cold.

"We have considered," said he, "the matter of which we were speaking recently, and under the peculiar circumstances in which we are placed, and in view of the fact that the success of our bill and the defeat of the Underground Steam Company is necessary for the protection of the best interests of the public and the facilitation of honest corporate business enterprise, I am empowered to authorize you to take such steps, Mr. Dowling, as seem to you desirable and requisite for the proper protection of our interests."

"Very good, sir. That is all that is necessary."

There was a brief silence, during which Mr. Barnstable joined his finger-tips together and looked at the fire. Then he rose augustly, and putting out his hand with a repellant gesture said, "There is one thing I insist on, which is that I shall know nothing of the details of this disagreeable business. I leave the matter wholly in your hands, Dowling."

"Oh, certainly, sir. And you may rely on my giving the cold shoulder to the rascals wherever it is possible for me to do so."

That is a pitiful story, is n't it? Virtue assaulted almost in its very temple, and given a black eye by sheer force of cruel, overwhelming circumstances. Yet a true story, and the prototype in its general features of a host of similar episodes occurring in the different cities of this

land of the free and the home of the brave.
Each case, of course, has its peculiar atmosphere. Not every leading villain has the sensitive and combative conscience of Thomas Barnstable; nor every general manager the bold, frank
style of Mr. Dowling. There is every phase of
soul-struggle and method from unblushing,
business-like bargain and sale to sphinx-like
and purposely unenlightened and ostrich-like
submission. In the piteous language of a de-
fender of Thomas Barnstable (not Josephine),
what can one do but submit? If one meets a
highwayman on the road, is one to be turned
back if a purse will secure a passage? Surely not
if the journey be of moment. Then is a corporate body (a corporation has no soul) to be
starved to death by delay and hostile legislation
if peace and plenty are to be had for an attorney's fee? If so, only the rascals would thrive
and honest corporations would bite the dust.
And so it happened that Mr. Dowling before
election cast his moral influence in favor of the
big four, and a little bird flew from headquarters with a secret message, couched in sufficiently vague language, to the effect that the
management would be pleased if the employees

of the People's Heat and Power Company were to mark crosses on their Australian ballots against the names of Peter Lynch, Jeremiah Dolan, Hon. William H. Bird, and the Hon. John P. Driscoll.

Let us allow the curtain to descend to slow music, and after a brief pause rise on some of our other characters. Behold now the fifty thousand respectable, well-intentioned, tolerably ignorant citizens who vote but are too busy with their own affairs to pay attention to politics, and as a consequence generally vote the party ticket or vote to please a friend. As a sample take Mr. John Baker, amiable and well-meaning physician, a practical philanthropist and an intelligent student of science by virtue of his active daily professional labors. For a week before election he is apt to have a distressing, soul-haunting consciousness that a City Government is shortly to be chosen and that he must, as a free-born and virtue-loving citizen, vote for somebody. He remembers that during the year there has been more or less agitation in the newspapers concerning this or that individual connected with the aldermanic office, but he has forgotten names and is all at sea as to who is who or what is what. Two days before election he receives and puts aside a circular containing a list of the most desirable candidates, as indicated by the Reform Society, intending to peruse it, but he is called from home on one evening by professional demands, and on the other by tickets for the theatre, so election morning arrives without his having looked at it. He forgets that it is election day, and is reminded of the fact while on his way to visit his patients by noticing that many of his acquaintances seem to be walking in the wrong direction. He turns also at the spur of memory, and mournfully realizes that he has left the list at home. To return would spoil his professional day, so he proceeds to the polls, and, in the hope of wise enlightenment, joins the first sagacious friend he encounters. It happens, perhaps, to be Dowling.

"Ah," says Dr. Baker, genially, "you 're just the man to tell me whom to vote for. One vote does n't count for much, but I like to do my duty as an American citizen."

"It 's a pretty poor list," says Dowling, pathetically, drawing a paper from his pocket. "I believe, however, in accomplishing the best possible results under existing circumstances. If I thought the Reform candidates could be elected, I would vote for them and for them only; but it's equally important that the very worst men should be kept out. I am going to vote for the Reform candidates and for Lynch, Dolan, Bird, and Driscoll. They're capable and they have had experience. If they steal, they'll steal judiciously and that is something. Some of those other fellows would steal the lamp-posts and hydrants if they got the chance."

"All right," says Dr. Baker. "I'll take your word for it. Let me write those names down. I suppose that some day or other we shall get a decent City Government. I admit that I don't give as much consideration to such matters as I ought, but the days are only twenty-four hours long."

Then from the same company there is Mr. David Jones, hay and grain dealer, honest and a diligent, reputable business man. He harbors the amiable delusion that the free-born American citizen in the exercise of the suffrage has intuitive knowledge as to whom to vote for, and that in the long run the choice of the sovereign people is wise and satisfactory. He is ready to admit that political considerations should not control selection for municipal office, but he has a latent distrust of reformers as aristocratic self-seekers or enemies of popular government. For instance, the idea that he or any other American citizen of ordinary education and good moral character is not fit to serve on the school committee offends his patriotism.

"What's the matter with Lynch, anyway?" he asks on his way to the polls. "I see some of his political enemies are attacking him in the press. If he were crooked, some one would have found it out in ten years. I met him once and he talked well. He has no frills round his neck."

"Nor wheels in his head," answers a fellow-patriot, who wishes to get a street developed and has put his case in Lynch's hands.

"He shall have my vote," says the hay and grain dealer.

As for the twenty-five thousand hide-bound partisans, I will state to begin with, my optimistic correspondent, that if this drama were concerned with any election but a city election, their number would be larger. But these make up in unswerving fixity of purpose for any diminution of their forces due to municipal con-

siderations. They are content to have their
thinking done for them in advance by a packed
caucus, and they go to the polls snorting like
war-horses and eager to vindicate by their ballots the party choice of candidates, or meekly
and reverently prepared to make a criss-cross
after every R or D, according to their faith,
with the fatuous fealty of sheep. Bigotry and
suspicions, ignorance and easy-going willingness
to be led, keep their phalanx steady and a constant old guard for the protection of comedians
and villains.

In another corner of the stage stand the ten
thousand superior, self-centred souls who neglect to vote and despise politics—the mixed
corps of pessimists, impractical dreamers, careless idlers, and hyper-cultured world-disdainers,
who hold aloof, from one motive or another,
from contact with common life and a share in
its responsibilities—some on the plea that uni-
versal suffrage is a folly or a failure, some that
earth is but a vale of travail which concerns
little the wise or righteous thinker, some from
sheer butterfly or stupid idleness. Were they
to vote they would help to offset that no less
large body of suffragists—the active enemies of

order, the hoodlum, tobacco-spitting, woman-insulting, rum-drinking ruffian brigade. There are only left the ten thousand conscientious citizens, real patriots—a corporal's guard, amid the general optimistic sweep toward the polls. These mark their crosses with care against the names of the honest men and perhaps some of the pretty honest, only to read in the newspapers next morning that the big four have been returned to power and that the confidence of the plain and sovereign people in the disinterested conduct of their public servants has again been demonstrated.

"Ho, ho, ho," laugh the low comedians. "Mum 's the word." The faces of the big four are wreathed in self-congratulatory smiles. At the homes of Peter Lynch and Jeremiah Dolan, those experienced individuals without occupation, there are cakes and ale. It is a mistake to assume that because a citizen is an Alderman he is not human and amiably domestic in his tastes. Jeremiah loves the little Dolans and is no less fond of riding his children on his leg than Thomas Barnstable, or any of the leading villains. When their father looks happy in the late autumn, the children know that their

Christmas stockings will be full. Jeremiah is at peace with all the world and is ready to sit with slicked hair for his photograph, from which a steel (or is it steal?) engraving will shortly be prepared for the new City Government year-book, superscribed: "Jeremiah Dolan, Chairman of the Board of Aldermen." A framed enlargement of this will hang on one side of the fire-place, and an embroidered motto, "God Bless Our Home," on the other, and all will be well with the Dolans for another twelve months. In his own home Jeremiah is a man of few words on public matters. Not unnaturally his children believe him to be of the salt of the earth, and he lets it go at that, attending strictly to business without seeking to defend himself in the bosom of his family from the diatribes of reformers. Still, it is reasonable to assume that, under the fillip of the large majority rolled up in his favor, he would be liable to give vent to his sense of humor so far as to refer in the presence of his wife and children to the young man who was willing to become an Alderman while waiting to be Senator, as a T. Willy.

If you have read "The Hon. Peter Stirling,"

you will remember that the hero rose to political stature largely by means of attending to the needs of the district, befriending the poor and the helpless and having a friendly, encouraging word for his constituents, high or low. The American public welcomed the book because it was glad to see the boss vindicated by these human qualities, and to think that there was a saving grace of unselfish service in the composition of the average successful politician. It would be unjust to the ʼbig four were I not to acknowledge that they have been shrewd or human enough to pursue in some measure this affable policy, and that the neighborhood and the district in which they live recognize them as hustlers to obtain office, privileges, and jobs for the humble citizen wishing to be employed by or to sell something to the City Government. To this constituency the comparatively small tax levied seems all in the day's work, a natural incident of the principle that when a man does something, he ought to be paid for it. To them the distinction that public service is a trust which has no right to pecuniary profit beyond the salary attached, and a reasonable amount of stationery, seems to savor of the millennium and to suggest a lack of practical intelligence on the part of its advocates. They pay the lawyer and the doctor; why not the Alderman?

To *A Political Optimist.*
III.

I AM reminded by Josephine that I seem to be getting into the dumps, which does not befit one who claims to be an optimistic philosopher. The drama just set before you is not, I admit, encouraging as a national exhibit, and I can imagine that you are already impatient to retort that the municipal stage is no fair criterion of public life in this country. I can hear you assert, with that confident air of national righteousness peculiar to the class of blind patriots to which you belong, that the leading politicians of the nation disdain to soil their hands by contact with city politics. Yet there I take issue with you squarely, not as to the fact but as to the truth of the lofty postulate seething in your mind that the higher planes of political activity are free from the venal and debasing characteristics of municipal public service—from the influence of the money power operating on a low public standard of honesty.

Most of us—even philosophers like myself —try to cling to the fine theory that the legisla-

tors of the country represent the best morals
and brains of the community, and that the men
elected to public office in the councils of the
land have been put forward as being peculiarly
fitted to interpret and provide for our needs,
by force of their predominant individual virtues
and abilities. Most of us appreciate in our secret souls that this theory is not lived up to,
and is available only for Fourth of July or
other rhetorical purposes. Yet we dislike to dismiss the ideal as unattainable, even though we
know that actual practice is remote from it; and
patriots still, we go on asserting that this is our
method of choice, vaguely hoping, like the well-
intentioned but careless voter, that some day
we shall get a decent government, municipal,
state, national—that is decent from the standpoint of our democratic ideal. And there is another theory, part and parcel of the other,
which we try to cling to at the same time, that
our public representatives, though the obviously
ornamental and fine specimens of their several
constituencies, are after all only every-day
Americans with whom a host of citizens could
change places without disparagement to either.
In other words, that our theory of government is

government by the average, and that the average is remarkably high. This comfortable view induces many like yourself to wrap themselves round with the American flag and smile at destiny, sure that everything will result well with us sooner or later, and impatient of criticism or doubts. As a people we delight in patting ourselves on the back and dismissing our worries as mere flea-bites. The hard cider of our patriotism gets readily into the brain and causes us to deny fiercely or serenely, according to our dispositions, that anything serious is the matter.

Yet whatever Fourth of July orators may say to the contrary, the fact remains that the sorry taint of bargain and sale, of holding up on the political highway and pacification by bribery in one form or another, permeates to-day the whole of our political system from the lowest stratum of municipal public life to the councils which make Presidents and United States Senators. To be sure, the Alderman in his capacity of low comedian dictating terms to corporations seeking civic privileges is the most unblushing, and hence the most obviously flagrant case; but it is well recognized by all who are brought in contact with legislative bodies of any sort in the country that either directly or indirectly the machinery of public life is controlled by aggregations of capital working on the hungry, easy-going, or readily flattered susceptibilities of a considerable percentage of the members. Certainly our national and state assemblies contain many high-minded, honest, intellectually capable men, but they contain as many more who are either dishonest or are so ignorant and easily cajoled that they permit themselves to be the tools of leading villains. Those cognizant of what goes on behind the scenes on the political stage would perhaps deny that such men as our friend Thomas Barnstable or his agent, Dowling, attempt to dictate nominations to either branch of the legislature on the tacit understanding that a member thus supported is to advocate or vote for their measures, and by their denial they might deceive a real simon-pure philosopher. But this philosopher knows better, and so do you, my optimistic friend. It is the fashion, I am aware, among conservative people, lawyers looking for employment, bankers and solid men of affairs, to put the finger on the lips when this evil is broached and whisper, "Hush!" They admit confidentially the truth of it, but they say "Hush!

What's the use of stirring things up? It can't
do any good and it makes the public discon-
tented. It excites the populists." So there is perpetual mystery and the game goes on. Men who
wish things good or bad come reluctantly or will-
ingly to the conclusion that the only way to get
them is by paying for them. Not all pay cash.
Some obtain that which they desire by working
on the weaknesses of legislators; following them
into banks where they borrow money, getting
people who hold them in their employ or give
them business to interfere, asking influential
friends to press them. Every railroad corporation in the country has agents to look after its
affairs before the legislature of the State through
which it operates, and what some of those agents
have said and done in order to avert molestation
would, if published, be among the most interesting memoirs ever written. Who doubts that elec-
tions to the United States Senate and House of
Representatives are constantly secured by the
use of money among those who have the power
to bestow nominations and influence votes? It
is notorious, yet to prove it would be no less difficult than to prove that Peter Lynch, Alderman
for ten years without occupation, has received

bribes from his fellow-citizens. How are the vast sums of money levied on rich men to secure the success of a political party in a Presidential campaign expended? For stationery, postage stamps, and campaign documents? For torch-light processions, rallies, and buttons? Some of it, certainly. The unwritten inside history of the political progress of many of the favorite sons of the nation during the last forty years would make the scale of public honor kick the beam though it were weighted with the cherry-tree and hatchet of George Washington. In one of our cities where a deputation of city officials attended the funeral of a hero of the late war with Spain, there is a record of four hundred dollars spent for ice-cream. Presumably this was a transcript of petty thievery inartistically audited. But there are no auditings of the real use of the thousands of dollars contributed to keep a party in power or to secure the triumph of a politically ambitious millionaire.

[*Note.*—Josephine, who had been sitting lost in thought since the conclusion of the drama, and who is fond of problem plays, inquired at this point whether I consider the low comedians or the leading villains the most to blame for the existing state of things.

" It is a pertinent question, Josephine, and one not easily answered. What is your view of the matter?"

"I suppose," she answered, "as you have termed the bribers the leading villains, they are the worst. And I do think that the temptation must be very great among the class of men who are without fine sensibilities to let themselves become the tools of rich and powerful people, who, as you have indicated, can help them immensely in return for a vote. It is astonishing that those in the community who are educated, well-to-do citizens, should commit such sins against decency and patriotism."

"Yes, it seems astonishing, but their plea is pathetic, as I have already stated, and somewhat plausible. Suppose for a minute that I am Thomas Barnstable defending himself and see how eloquent I can be. 'What would you have me do, Madam? I am an honest man and my directors are honest men; the bills we ask for are always just and reasonable. I have never in my life approached a legislator with an improper offer, nor have I used direct or indirect bribery

so long as it was absolutely possible to avoid
doing so. But when a gang of cheap and cunning tricksters block the passage of my corporation's measures, and will not let them become
law until we have been bled, I yield as a last re-
sort. We are at their mercy. It is a detestable
thing to do, I admit, but it is necessary if we are
to remain in business. There is no alternative.
The responsibility is on the dishonest and incapable men whom the American public elects
to office, and who under the specious plea of pro-
tecting the rights of the plain people levy black-
mail on corporate interests. Corporations do not
wish to bribe, but they are forced to do so in
self-defence.' There! Is not that a tear-compel-
ling statement?"

"I can see your side," said Josephine.

"Pardon me," I interrupted. "It is Mr. Barnstable's side, not mine. I am not a capitalist, only
a philosopher."

"Well, his side then; and I feel sorry for him
in spite of the weakness of his case. Only his
argument does not explain the others. I should
not suppose that men like Mr. Prendergast could
truthfully declare that all the legislation they ask
for is just and reasonable."

"Precisely. Yet they buy their desires in the open market from the free-born representatives of the people. If any one states so at the time he is hushed up, if possible; if not, there is an investigation, nothing is proved, and the integrity of the legislative body is vindicated. I can shed a tear on behalf of men like Mr. Barnstable, a crocodile tear, yet still a tear. But there is the larger army of hard-headed, dollar-hunting, practical capitalists, who are not forming corporations for their health, so to speak, to be reckoned with. My eloquence is palsied by them. They would tell you that they were obliged to bribe, but they do not waste much time in resistance or remorse. They seem to regard the evil as a national custom, unfortunate and expensive, but not altogether inconvenient. Confidentially over a cigar they will assure you that the French, the Spanish, the Turks, and the Chinese are infinitely worse and that this is merely a passing phase of democracy, whatever that may mean."

"Dreadful," said Josephine. "And then there are the people with money who aid and abet their own nominations for Congress. I think I could mention some of them."

"Well, you must n't. It might hurt their feelings, for they may not know exactly what was done except in a general way. After all is over they ask 'how much?' draw a check and make few inquiries. That is the genteel way. But in some states it is not necessary or politic to be genteel. The principle is the same, but the process is less subtle and aristocratic. But have n't you a word of extenuation to offer on behalf of the low comedians? Think of Jeremiah Dolan and the little Dolans."

"I suppose he also would say it was n't true," said Josephine.

"Oh, yes. 'Lady, there is n't a word of truth in the whole story. Some one 's been stuffing you.'"

"They must be dreadfully tempted, poor wretches."

"'Lady, it 's all make-believe. But it 's one thing to talk and another to sit still and have a fellow whisper in your ear that you have only to vote his way to get five thousand in clean bills and no questions asked. When a man has a mortgage on his house to pay, five thousand would come in handy. I 'm only supposing, Lady, and no one can prove I took a cent.'"

"Fred," said Josephine, after a solemn pause, "the dreadful thought has just occurred to me that the American people may not be—are not strictly honest."

"Sh!" I shouted eagerly and seizing a tea table-cloth I threw it over her head and stayed her speech.

"My dear, do you realize what you are saying?"

"Do you realize that you are tumbling my hair?"

I paid no heed to this unimportant interjection, but said, "If any true patriot were to hear you make such an accusation you would subject yourself and me to some dreadful punishment, such as happened to Dreyfus, or 'The Man Without a Country.' Not honest? By the shades of George Washington, what are you thinking of? Why, one of the chief reasons of our superiority to all the other nations of the world is because of our honesty—our immunity from the low moral standards of effete, frivolous despotisms and unenlightened masses who are without the blessings of freedom. Not strictly honest? Josephine, your lack of tact, if nothing else, is positively audacious. Do you

expect me to break this cruel piece of news to
the optimistic patriot to whom this letter is ad-
dressed?"

"I think you are silly," said my wife, freeing
herself from the tea table-cloth and trying to
compose her slightly disordered tresses. "I only
thought aloud, and I said merely what you
would have said sooner or later in more philosophical terms. I saw that you were tempted
by the fear of not seeming a patriot to dilly-
dally with the situation and avoid expressing
yourself in perspicuous language. T-h-i-e-f
spells thief; b-r-i-b-e-r-y spells bribery. I don't
know much about politics, and I'm not a philosopher, but I understand the meaning of every-day English, and I should say that we were
not even pretty honest. There! Those are my
opinions, and I think you will save time if you
send them in your letter instead of beating about
the bush for extenuating circumstances. If you
don't, I shall—for really, Fred, it's too simple
a proposition. And as for the blame, it's six of
one and half a dozen of the other."

"Josephine, Josephine," I murmured, "there
goes my last chance of being sent to the Phi-
lippines, in my capacity as a philosopher, to

study whether the people of those islands are fit for representative government."]

You have read what Josephine says, my optimistic friend. She has stated that she would write to you her summing up of the whole matter if I did not, so I have inserted her deduction in all its crudity. She declares the trouble to be that the American people are dishonest. Of course, I cannot expect you to agree with any such conclusion, and I must admit that the boldness of the accusation is a shock to my own sensibilities as a patriot. Of course, Josephine is a woman and does not understand much about politics and ways and means, and it is notorious that women jump at conclusions instead of approaching them logically and in a dignified manner. But it is also said that their sudden conclusions are apt to be right. Dishonest? Dear me, what a dreadful suggestion. I really think that she went a little too far. And yet I am forced to agree that appearances are very much against us, and that if we hope to lead the world in righteousness and progress we must, to recur to political phraseology, mend our moral fences. I do not indulge in meteoric flights, like

Josephine. Let us argue the matter out soberly.

You and I, as men of the world, will agree that if the American people prefer or find it more serviceable to cherish bribery as a federal institution, no one will interfere. The fact that it is ethically wrong is interesting to real philosophers and to the clergy, but bribery will continue to flourish like a bay-tree if it is the sort of thing which the American people like. Now, to all outward appearances they find it, if not grateful and comforting, at least endurable and convenient. Certainly, except among the class of people whom you would be apt to stigmatize as "holier than thous," there is comparatively little interest taken in the question. The mass of the community seek refuge behind the agreeable fiction that the abuse does n't exist or exists only in such degree as to be unimportant. Many of these people know that this is false, but they will not admit that they think so in order not to make such doings familiar, just as their custom is to speak of legs as lower limbs in order not to bring a blush to the cheek of the young person. For thorough-going hypocrisy—often unconscious, but still hypocrisy—

no one can equal a certain kind of American. It is so much easier in this world, where patting on the back is the touch-stone of preferment and popularity, to think that everything is as serene as the surface indicates, though you are secretly sure that it is not. How much more convenient to be able to say truthfully, "I have no knowledge of the facts, so don't bother me," than to be constantly wagging the head and entertaining doubts concerning the purity of one's fellow-citizens, and so making enemies.

As I have indicated earlier in this letter, the ideal is dear to our patriotic sensibilities that we are governed by average opinion, and that the average is peculiarly high. The fastidious citizen in this country has been and still is fond of the taunt that men of upright character and fine instincts—what he calls gentlemen—will not enter public life, for the reason that they will not eat dirt. The reply has been that the real bugaboo of the fastidious citizen is one of manners, and that in the essentials of character, in strong moral purpose and solid worth, the average American voter is the peer of any aristocracy. The issue becomes really one of fact, and mere solemn assertion will not serve as evidence beyond a certain point. If the majority prefer dishonesty, the power is in their hands to perpetuate the system ; but believing as you and I do that the majority at heart is honest, how are we to explain the continued existence of the evil ? How as patriots shall we reconcile the perpetuation in power of the low comedians, Peter Lynch and Jeremiah Dolan, except on the theory that it is the will of the majority that they should continue to serve the people ? This is not a question of kid gloves, swallow-tailed coats, and manners, but an indictment reflecting on the moral character and solid worth of the nation. How are we to explain it ? What are we to say ? Can we continue to declare that we are the most honest and aspiring people in the world and expect that portion of the world which has any sense of humor not to smile ? Are we, who have been accustomed to boast of our spotless integrity as a people, ready to fall back on and console ourselves with the boast, which does duty nowadays on lenient lips, that we are as honest as any of the nations of Europe except, possibly, England ? That is an indirect form of patriotic negation under the shadow of which low comedians and leading vil-

lains could ply their trade comparatively unmo-
lested.

As a philosopher, who is not a real philosopher, I find this charge of Josephine's a difficult
nut to crack, and I commend it respectfully to
your attention to mull over at your leisure, trust-
ing that it may temper the effulgence of your
thoughts on Independence Day. Yet having had
my say as a philosopher, let me as an optimist,
willing to succor a fellow-optimist, add a few considerations indicating that the situation may not
be so ultimately evil as the existing state of affairs and Josephine would have us believe. I write
"may not be," because I am not altogether confident that my intelligence is not being cajoled
by the natural cheeriness and buoyancy of my
disposition. The sole question at issue is whether
the majority of the American people are really
content to have the money power of the country
prey upon and be the prey of the lowest moral
sense of the community.

We have before us an everyday spectacle of
eager aggregations of capital putting aside scruples as visionary and impractical, and hence "un-
American," in order to compass success, and at
the other side of the counter the so-called repre-

sentatives of the people, solemn in their verbiage but susceptible to occult and disgraceful influences. The two parties to the intercourse are discreet and business-like, and there is little risk of tangible disclosure. Practically aloof from them, except for a few moments on election day, stand the mass of American citizens busy with their own money-getting or problem-solving, and only too ready to believe that their representatives are admirable. They pause to vote as they pause to snatch a sandwich at a railroad station. "Five minutes for refreshments!" Five minutes for political obligations! Individually there are thousands of strictly honest and noble-hearted men in the United States. Who doubts it? The originality and strength of the American character is being constantly manifested in every field of life. But there we speak of individuals; here we are concerned with majorities and the question of average morality and choice. For though we have an aspiring and enlightened van of citizens to point the way, you must remember that emigration and natural growth has given us tens of thousands of ignorant, prejudiced, and sometimes unscrupulous citizens, each of whose votes counts one. Perhaps it is true—and here is my grain of consolation or hope—that the average voter is so easy-going, so long-suffering, so indisposed to find fault, so selfishly busy with his own affairs, so proud of our institutions and himself, so afraid of hurting other people's feelings, and so generally indifferent as to public matters, provided his own are serene, that he chooses to wink at bribery if it be not in plain view, and likes to deceive himself into believing that there is nothing wrong. The long and short of it seems to be that the average American citizen is a good fellow, and in his capacity of good fellow cannot afford to be too critical and particular. He leaves that to the reformer, the literary man, the dude, the college professor, the mugwump, the philosopher, and other impractical and un-American people. If so, what has become of that heritage of his forefathers, the stern Puritan conscience? Swept away in the great wave of material progress which has centred all his energies on what he calls success, and given to the power of money a luring importance which is apt to make the scruples of the spirit seem unsubstantial and bothersome. An easy-going, trouble-detesting, self-absorbed democracy between the buffers of rapacity and rascality.

A disagreeable conclusion for an optimist, yet less gloomy than the other alternative. This condition admits of cure, for it suggests a torpid conscience rather than deliberate acquiescence. It indicates that the representatives are betraying the people, and that there is room for hope that the people eventually may rise in their might and call them to account. If they do, I beg as a philosopher with humorous proclivities, to caution them against seizing the wrong pig by the ear. Let them fix the blame where it belongs, and not hold the corporations and the money power wholly responsible. It may be possible in time to abolish trusts and cause rich men sleepless nights in the crusading name of populism, but that will avail little unless at the same time they go to the real root of the matter, and quicken the average conscience and strengthen the moral purpose of the plain people of the United States. There will be leading villains and low comedians so long as society permits, and so long as the conscience of democracy is torpid. The players in the drama are, after all, only the people themselves. Charles the First was beheaded because he betrayed the liberties of the people. Alas! there is no such remedy for a corrupt democracy, for its heads are like those of Hydra, and it would be itself both the victim and the executioner.

THE END

www.ingramcontent.com/pod-product-compliance
Lightning Source LLC
Chambersburg PA
CBHW020114030726
47498CB00006B/2092